Other Novels by
J.R. Stoddard

COUGAR HUNT
COUGAR CAMP

Lauren enjoy,
To Enjoy
J.R. Stoddard

COUGAR CANYON

By

J.R. STODDARD
A Buck Logan Suspense Novel

Cougar   Publishing

Cougar Publishing
Olympia, Washington

Library of Congress
Cataloging-in-Publication Data
Stoddard, J. R.
Cougar Canyon/ J.R. Stoddard
    p.cm
ISBN: 978-0-9701401-3-5

Cover Design by Kathy Campbell

FIRST EDITION, 2008

Manufactured in the United States of America

To my father
Robert Ray Stoddard

Who taught me the wonders of nature
through numerous camping, fishing,
hunting, and hiking trips.

Many thanks to my loving wife and best friend of twenty-nine years for all of her support, proofing and editing.

1

After a long, stressful work week it was finally Friday. Traffic was light and Jane Gray was home within twenty minutes. Anxious to get going on her weekend visit she changed her clothes and made a sandwich to eat on the trip to her parents house, the house where she had grown up. Mentally checking off her list of items needed she was glad she packed the night before. From experience she was less apt to forget something if she wasn't rushed after she returned home from work. Jane was ready to depart just before six.

She got into her new SUV and carefully backed down the driveway. She stopped and pressed the button on the remote attached to the sun visor to close the garage door. She sat there waiting until the door had completely closed. When she was sure the door was closed she continued out into the street and drove away. She drove across Newtown to the I-90 freeway and headed east up into the Cascade Mountains.

It was a beautiful spring evening and the scenery was breathtaking. The deciduous trees were beginning to turn out new leaves. The mountains, with all their majestic peaks, were a wall of green from the freeway all the way up to the top. Passing over the Snoqualmie River she looked to the south and saw a man and woman standing in the river swinging their rods up and down, playing their flies toward the hungry trout. That looks like fun she thought to herself, I'll have to try it someday. In spite of the noise, Jane had her window down enjoying the fresh air and the heavenly smell of the evergreens. Their cones were putting out volumes of pollen which coated vehicles every day with a blanket of yellow and filled the air with magnificent fragrances. The pollen was so thick she could draw pictures on the hood of her car after it sat in the parking lot all day while she was at work.

A graduate of Washington State University in bio-engineering she had landed a great job with an upstart bio-tech company shortly after she graduated three years ago. She had saved enough money to put a down payment on a house in Newtown and had moved into it three months ago. By Newtown standards it was small house, only 1200 square feet, three bedrooms, two baths, but was plenty big enough for a single woman. The back yard of the house bordered a wide-open area used as a watershed. It was essentially a small canyon at the base of the mountains and was left natural except for the trails that ran along side the stream that meandered along the bottom of the canyon.

After she passed Snoqualmie Summit and headed down the east side of the mountains the lush green scenery along the freeway slowly turned to sparsely treed areas. The ground was covered with wild flowers; poppies, lupine, wild daisies, fireweed and many others. This was her favorite time of year, enjoying the scenery as she zipped along at seventy miles an hour. Jane hadn't been home to the family farm for months. Working seven days a week for the last month to finish a project, she was more than ready for some rest.

She took the off-ramp at exit one fifty-four in the dark and headed north. At precisely eight-thirty she drove up the long driveway to the old farmhouse that had been in her family for three generations. When she was in high school she decided she was not going to be a farmer or a farmer's wife, but she still loved to come home to visit and spend a few days driving the tractor or listening to the sheep 'baa' in the meadow.

When she opened the car door there was Bit, their little black and white sheep dog, waiting for her, tail wagging.

"Hi Bit!" excited to see him she took both sides of his face in her hands and rubbed his head, then gave him a big hug. His tail flew back and forth, obviously glad to see her.

"Hi honey," Judy, her mother, gave her a big hug. "How was the traffic?"

"Hi mom," looking around, "the traffic was great, not even a slow down anywhere." Hugging her in return with a kiss on the cheek. "Where's dad?"

"He's in the barn working on the thrashing machine. Let's put your things in the house and then go get him. It's time for him to come in anyway."

Bit followed them into the house and up to Jane's old bedroom.

"It's so nice to have you home again. It's been too long."

"It's only been a few months mom. I finally finished the project so I got a whole weekend off."

"You work too many hours at that place."

"Ha, that's a good one. Look at dad, it's nine o'clock and he's still out in the barn working. I bet he started working by eight this morning. On a farm you work seven days a week and the work is never done."

Sighing, Judy slowly nodded her head. "Yep, you're right about that dear."

"Let's go get dad and have a piece of pie. I made an apple pie this afternoon because I know it's your favorite."

Just thinking about her mom's homemade apple pie got her appetite going.

Paul was so focused on the thrashing machine that he didn't hear them come up on him.

"Hi dad."

Paul dropped the wrench and turned around. Wrapping his arms around his daughter he gave her a big hug and a kiss on the cheek, "Hi honey."

"Come on Paul, let's go have some apple pie. The thrasher can wait until tomorrow."

Linking her arm through her dad's on the way back to the house Jane said, "Why don't you buy a new one. You're always working on that thing. It's ancient."

"This is a big wheat farm and big farms take big machines, they're expensive."

They talked until eleven and decided it was time to hit the hay. Bit took his usual place next to Jane's bed when she was there. When Jane wasn't there Bit slept outside, usually on the front porch.

Shortly after three in the morning all hell broke loose in the sheep pen. It was Paul's routine to herd them all in from the meadow near the house before dark and put them in the pen for the night.

Paul jumped out of bed and hurriedly dressed, grabbing his old Winchester 30-30 lever action rifle from the gun rack at the back door and a flashlight on his way out. He flipped on the back-porch light and jogged out to the barn. There was not a sound coming from the open pen which was surrounded by a five foot high railing on three sides and the barn on the fourth side. He could hear something moving through the wheat field off toward the west. In the pen he found five dead sheep. Each one had a broken neck. There was no blood or any other sign of trauma, just the broken necks. The sixth sheep was nowhere to be seen.

"Cougar," knowingly he whispered to himself while shining the light around the fence.

At the breakfast table Paul told them what had happened. "Last month Jay Miller up the road had two sheep killed the same way. He called the fish and wildlife enforcement officer and was told that if it came back he could shoot it. A lot of help that was, now it's done it again."

"What are you going to do?" Jane asked.

"I'll have to stay up tonight and see if it comes back. I'll leave all the carcasses out there, they're no good now anyway. I may have to do it for a few days to see if it's going to come back."

"I'll call Andy and let them know there's a cougar roaming around," Jane's mother said. "We don't want our grandchildren getting hurt, they're not much more than a stones throw away."

"Good idea, maybe he'll come over tonight and help me stake it out. Staying awake all night will be tough."

Andy, Jane's brother, and his family came over for dinner that night. It was getting dark as they finished. Paul grabbed his rifle and he and Andy headed out the back door. On the way to the barn Andy stopped at his pickup truck and took his rifle from the rack across the window behind the seat.

They climbed the ladder to the hayloft and opened the loading door on the north side of the big barn. After pushing bales of hay over to the opening to provide some concealment they each sat down on a bale of hay at either side of the door.

"Guess we just wait now," Andy said.

"Yep, could be a long night."

"Yeah, but I don't like the idea of a cougar hanging around, with the kids and all," Andy replied.

"That's for sure. Don't need our grandchildren getting hurt, or anyone else for that matter. I don't like the idea of it killing all my sheep either. This is at least the second time it has killed sheep. Who knows how long it's been hanging around the farm, checking out the livestock, and maybe people too."

They were both half dozing at three when the big cat jumped over the fence into the pen. Andy was first to notice the movement, nudging his dad. Quietly they lifted their rifles. The cougar took one of the sheep firmly between its massive jaws and dragged it over to the fence.

It could easily clear the fence carrying the hundred pound sheep. It crouched to jump.

The quiet country night rang with the loud discharge of the two rifles in close succession.

Andy started to get up. Paul put his hand on Andy's arm to stop him.

"Let's sit here and watch it for a few minutes, just to be sure it stays down. Cats have nine lives and some predatory animals can tear you apart when they've been wounded."

"Good idea," Andy replied. "Remember a few years ago when I got kicked by the deer I thought was dead. My leg hurt for weeks."

Five minutes later the big cat jumped up and looked straight up into the loft, then crouched down.

"Whoa," Andy yelled out, quickly raising his rifle. Paul already had his rifle up and fired, hitting it at the base of the neck, dropping it immediately.

Ten minutes later when it had not moved they went down and slit it's throat quickly, just to make sure it wouldn't jump up again.

Andy checked out the big cat. Inspecting the teats he said, "Look, it's a nursing mother. I wonder how many kittens she has."

"Sure is," Paul agreed. "We'll probably never know how many kittens she has. They're probably well hidden in a cave or someplace. Most likely they'll starve to death since they're still nursing. We might as well get the small tractor and bury them all at the same time."

"Go ahead and get it, I'll drag them all out the gate."

They worked together to lift the dead cougar and sheep, into the bucket of the tractor and then drove them out in the field to bury them.

"Well, at least we won't have to worry about the kids now. Too bad about the sheep though," Andy said when they'd finished.

Sunday morning Jane and her mother sat at the breakfast table. "From all the shots I heard last night they must have got the cougar," Jane questioned.

"Yes they did. Dad said it was a big one too. They had a hard time lifting it up into the tractor bucket. He said it probably weighed about a hundred fifty pounds."

"Wow, that's a big kitty."

After they'd finished the dishes Jane said, "I think I'll take the small tractor and disk the lower field so it's read for dad to plant."

"Fine by me, I'm sure dad will be happy to have the help. Be back by noon for lunch, okay? Dad should be up before long so we can get the whole story."

"Thanks for the breakfast," Jane gave her mother a hug and headed for the back door. "See you at noon."

The tractor started right up and she let the clutch out slowly, inching the throttle arm up gradually until it was moving at a comfortable speed. She smiled as she looked at the wheat on her left side. The tractor rocked from side to side as she traveled along the rutted dirt road. The green seemed to go on forever, waving back and forth with the gentle breeze.

She thought about James Taylor's song "The Walking Man Walks on By," the way the wheat waved in the breeze, it looked like the field was walking. Memories of her childhood flowed through her, it was a good feeling. She also loved the freedom of being by herself out in the field.

It took about ten minutes for Jane to reach the unplanted field. Weeds were beginning to grow in places. She stopped and reached over with her left hand and lowered the disks. Letting out the clutch, she adjusted the depth of the disk as the tractor slowly plodded forward under the heavy load of all the earth that was being disked up to displace the weeds, and at the same time aerate the soil. The next step would be to plant the field using a series of small plows that opened the soil, then dropped seeds into the track and cover up the opening, all at the same time. After that the farmer prayed for rain. It usually took a good four to six days of at least a small amount of rain for the seeds to germinate and survive. Timing was critical in farming.

Two hours later she was on her fourth trip around the field. She paralleled a ditch that was always left natural because it was too difficult to plow. Out of the corner of her eye she saw something moving in the bushes near the edge where the brush stopped and the plowed field began. She put the clutch in gently and the forward movement stopped dead. She watched as a baby cougar emerged from hiding. Putting the tractor in neutral, she sat there and watched the kitten in awe. She'd never seen a cougar in the wild before.

"Oh my god, I'll bet that was your mother they shot last night."

She got down from the tractor and slowly walked toward it with careful steps. The kitten 'meowed' a mournful cry. It looked like it was only a few weeks old. She knelt down and the kitten moved toward her, rubbing against her leg. Jane ran her hand across its back and it pressed harder against her leg.

She sat down and gently picked up the spotted cat and held it in her lap. "Well, I can't leave you out here to die," she said out loud, "and that's surely what will happen."

She slowly got up, cradling the kitten in her arms, and walked over to the tractor. Holding the kitten in her lap, she put the tractor in gear, raised the disk and headed back to the farmhouse. The kitten remained surprisingly calm for the entire ride. It apparently sensed that something was wrong.

As she drove up to the barnyard Paul could see she had something in her lap by the way she was sitting. When Jane was growing up she had brought home all kinds of critters; baby rabbits, birds, even a baby raccoon once. The raccoon actually turned out to be a good pet until it was about two years old and it just disappeared one night. He was accustomed to her propensity to nurture orphaned animals. He met her when she climbed down from the tractor, then he realized what it was.

"Why in tarnation did you bring that dang thing back here?"

"I found it out in the draw."

"Here, give it to me and I'll take care of it."

Alarmed, she clutched the kitten in close to her chest. "What do you mean by 'take care of it'?" she asked, already knowing the answer.

"Drown it, what else? That's what you do with cats you don't want."

"You can't do that. It's just a baby."

"Cats are always cute when they are kittens. They grow up. That's the problem. Look what it's mother did to our sheep."

"No way, I'm taking it home."

Paul shook his head, "That's a bad idea, but I've never been able to change your mind once you've decided to do something. I know better than to even try to talk you out of it. In a few months, it'll be tearing your house apart and eating you out of house and home. When it gets bigger, it will become too dangerous to have around. It won't take long for you to realize it's a bad idea."

Bit went nuts when he saw the kitten. He was used to cats, there were plenty of loose ones around the barn all the time. Some were friendly to him and people, some were more wild. He sniffed at the new kitten, this one was clearly different.

Jane took the kitten over to an enclosure in a corner inside the barn that Paul had helped her build for the baby raccoon she had brought home many years ago. It had housed many baby animals she'd brought home while growing up. Jane looked around the barn until she

found the old bottle and nipple used to
feed newborn animals around the farm when
the mother was having trouble. She went
to the storage room where supplies were
kept and got some of the powdered formula
that was used when farm animal babies
were in need of help. She put some in the
bottle and then went to the deep sink
where she filled it up with water.

She went into the house and heated the
bottle in the microwave then returned to
the barn. When she opened the enclosure
the kitten was right there ready to get
out. She took the kitten and sat on a
bale of hay, cradling it in her lap and
squeezed a few drops from the nipple onto
the kitten's muzzle. The kitten licked
its muzzle and then Jane pressed the
nipple to her mouth until it began
licking the nipple. It wasn't long before
the kitten eagerly took it in its mouth
and began sucking. All the while Bit
stood next to Jane, occasionally letting
out a muffled growl. Some of it was
probably his displeasure of Jane's
attention being focused on a cat, an
intruder at that. He could tell that this
one was not like all the other cats
around the barn. It just smelled
different.

After an early Sunday dinner saying 'good
bye' was a tearful event. Her mother and
father stood in the circular loop in
front of the farmhouse waving as Jane
pulled away. She looked in the rearview
mirror and could see her father shaking
his head. The kitten jumped around inside

the car, from back to front, but by the
time she merged into the traffic on I-90
the kitten had found a comfortable place
curled up on her lap. Jane stroked her
back and she began to purr. She would
later find out, from studying everything
she could find on cougars, they are the
smallest of all the big cats, and are the
only big cats that purr.

Cruising up the mountain she wondered
what she would name the kitten. She
thought, 'I don't even know if it's a
male or female'. As she stroked it she
raised the tail, quickly glancing between
the road and the cat. She didn't see any
testicles so she thought she'd take a
chance and assume it was a female. The
cat looked up at her with brilliant blue
eyes, glistening in the dying light. As
she passed Lake Easton a light mist began
hitting the windshield and she switched
the wipers on. That solved she settled on
'Misty.'

Cresting the top of the mountain she
looked up the hill to the south and saw
the ski lifts sitting there idle. There
was still plenty of snow, but the chairs
were empty. The preceding four months had
provided the skiers with an opportunity
to enjoy nature and the beauty of the
mountains, blanketed in white. The
branches of the trees laden with snow
along the ski trails provided the winter
wonderland views for those fortunate
enough to be able to afford the sport and
adventurous enough to endure the cold.
When spring arrived the hardy lot had
found new challenges to pursue.

There had been plenty of cats around when Jane was growing up, but none had been in the house. They had all lived in and around the barn. They had a purpose, to keep the mouse and rat population under control. Since she wouldn't be able to let this cat out to run free, she needed to make plans. Making a mental note she came up with, kitty litter, a cat box, cat food, something to play with, a scratching post, and a bed to sleep in.

She exited I-90 to Newtown and soon turned up her street. She pressed the remote control for the garage door opener two houses away and by the time she drove into her driveway the door was all the way up. She drove right into the garage and pressed the button to close the door. She didn't want to take a chance on Misty taking off on a sightseeing tour of the neighborhood so she waited for the garage door to close before she opened her car door. Misty jumped out immediately, happy to be free of the confines of the car. The kitten explored the new curiosities of the garage while Jane unloaded the car. Jane left the door into the house open and soon Misty followed her in to explore her new habitat. Jane finished unloading the SUV then sat down on the sofa and made up a shopping list. Misty had found a tennis ball and was busy batting it about and chasing it. Jane watched the cougar kitten for a few minutes then added kitten toys to the list.

"Okay Misty, I have to go to the store. You behave yourself while I'm gone."

She got up and headed for the door to the garage with Misty close in trail. Jane put her foot out to keep Misty from following her into the garage. Two hours later she returned from the grocery store with over a hundred dollars worth of cat food and other supplies.

She placed the cat box in a corner of the kitchen and filled it with litter. Next she mixed some baby formula with water, put it into the microwave and nuked it for thirty seconds. When it was sufficiently warm she put it into a baby bottle. The kitten followed her around relentlessly. Jane sat down on the sofa and the kitten snuggled up nosing the bottle. Jane squeezed it gently causing a drop to emerge from the tip. The kitten licked the drop, then began licking more as Jane gently pressed the nipple into Misty's mouth. The bottle was empty in less than two minutes. Jane repeated the process three times until the kitten, sated, stretched it's hind legs and promptly fell asleep with her head on Jane's lap.

It was getting late and Jane had to go to work the next day. She slipped away, leaving Misty asleep on the sofa, and went upstairs to her room. She took a quick shower and crawled into bed, thinking about the events of the day.

At six a.m. the clock radio came on and Boss Scaggs was singing 'My Home Town.' Jane's nose perceived a new odor.

She slowly opened her eyes to find Misty's muzzle facing her four inches away, head on the pillow, sound asleep. She reached over and stroked the kitten from head to tail. Misty stretched her hind legs and relaxed, still asleep. Jane rolled over pushing the blankets away and put her feet on the floor, searching for her slippers, rubbing the sleep out of her eyes. Her brain was saying, 'I need coffee.'

She headed for the kitchen in a semi-conscious state and filled the coffee pot with water from the Brita water filter container. Still sleepy-eyed she yawned, then poured it into the coffee maker, placed a filter in the basket and scooped two measures of coffee grounds into the basket and touched the 'on' button.

When she smelled the coffee in the works she headed for the shower, the hot water cascaded over her body awakening her. The smell of the natural peppermint Castle soap invigorated her, the tingling woke her up. Misty had heard her moving around and was up now laying next to the shower door watching as she lathered up.

Jane got out of the shower and toweled off as Misty observed. She put on a robe and went to the kitchen, poured a cup of coffee for herself, then fixed a bottle of formula for Misty. She sat on the sofa, coffee in her right hand and Misty laying at her left sucking the bottle and both watched the morning news. After a second bottle and another cup of coffee Jane returned to her bedroom, Misty romping around behind her. She dressed quickly, shaped and blow dried her hair in the bathroom, then applied her makeup. All the while Misty sat in the bathroom keenly watching her every move.

Finally ready to leave for work Jane went to the kitchen, giving Misty a smooth stroke across the head, along the back, and caressing her tail to the end. She filled a travel mug with coffee and looked over at Misty.

"See you tonight," she said and exited the door from the kitchen to the garage.

When Jane returned that evening Misty heard the garage door opening. She jumped up from the sofa and ran to the kitchen, sitting in the center of the kitchen floor, watching the door to the garage. Jane was surprised as she opened the door from the garage into the kitchen to see Misty anxiously waiting, tail swinging back and forth.

Misty watched as Jane walked in and set her work for the night on the counter. Misty casually walked over to Jane and pushed at her leg for attention, purring. Jane reached down and stroked Misty with her left hand.

"Hi there, did you miss me today?"

She could tell that Misty was hungry so she fixed a bottle of formula and a hot chocolate for herself and went into the living room. Sitting on the sofa Misty jumped up next to her and went right for the bottle. It was empty before Jane had a chance to take a sip of her hot chocolate.

"I wish they made these bottles bigger," talking out loud, "I should have brought one home from the farm," she mused, returning to the kitchen for a refill. She poured the dry mix into a quart container then filled it up with water. After shaking it vigorously she filled the baby bottle and placed it in the microwave. As it heated, she put the remaining mix in the refrigerator to be used later.

After Misty had consumed four bottles she stretched out and quickly fell asleep. Jane sat on the sofa stroking her for a half hour before getting up to make some dinner.

Two months later Jane returned from work one evening with a new installment of cat things. She carried a twenty five pound bag of cat food into the kitchen. Misty was now ready to go off the bottle and eat regular cat food. Jane filled one side of the new double sided bowl with water and placed it on the floor, filling the other side with fish flavored dry cat food. Misty took a sniff. Jane picked out a single piece and rubbed it across her muzzle until Misty opened her mouth. Jane slid it in and Misty immediately began to chew it. Five minutes later the bowl was empty.

Laughing, "I guess I should have expected that!" She filled it back up again. After refilling the bowl twice, Misty seemed to have had enough.

The next problem was to make a new cat box. Misty had grown too big to use the store bought litter box made for house cats. Jane went out to the garage, with Misty following her, and removed two 2x4's from the roof of her SUV. She laid them on the floor of the garage then removed a sheet of Plexiglas from the back of the SUV. Measuring the plastic carefully she then measured off forty-eight inches per side on the 2x4's. She removed a hand saw from the wall and cut the wood, then nailed the four pieces together in a square. She applied caulk to the top of the box all the way around and then set the Plexiglas on top. She moved it around to spread the caulk and then placed partially filled one gallon paint cans on the glass corners to secure it in place until the caulk set.

The next morning Jane went to the garage and checked the new litter box. It seemed to be well set. She went to pick it up, but it was cumbersome and heavy. Using her farm girl skills, she hoisted it up and rested the side on her shoulder, holding the corner in her left hand. It was still a challenge but she managed to half carry, half drag it to the basement. She set it down in the corner and poured four large bags of cat litter into the new box. She then dumped the old cat litter box into the corner of the new box to give Misty the scent that this now was the place to go.

The cat urine had a very pungent and uniquely distinct odor. Unlike house cats which would urinate four to eight ounces of urine a day, a cougar could expel

twenty to more than thirty ounces a day.
The air mover for the heat pump, which
heated and cooled the house was in the
basement. Whenever the heater came on it
saturated the house with the pungent
aroma of Misty's urine. No amount of
deodorizing had any effect. Jane had to
scoop the wet litter out every night when
she got home from work and dump it over
the edge of the watershed. The result was
that the deer stayed well away from her
back yard.

Misty had the run of the house while Jane
was at work. She slept most of the day
and was ready to play when Jane came
home. One evening when Misty was about
six months old Jane returned from work to
find her new sofa torn to shreds. She sat
down and cried.
     "What am I going to do with you? I
can't have you tearing the house apart."

The following day, a Saturday, she headed
to the hardware store after breakfast.
She had a long list, and returned home
shortly before noon, satisfied that she
could find a solution. She removed the
ten foot long 4x4 from the roof rack and
carried it down to the basement, setting
it on the floor. When one grows up on a
farm one learns to do whatever needs to
be done. Having helped her father repair
anything from the barn door to a tractor
she studied the floor joists, then got a
ladder and measuring tape, taking the
measurement from the top of the joist to
the floor. She cut off the 4x4 so that it

just fit from the basement floor to the bottom of the plywood floor of the upstairs. Taking a piece of carpet left over from when the house was new, she wrapped it around the 4x4. She then nailed one side down the length of the pole and stretched the other end around, overlapping the first piece and nailed it to the 4x4. She put the pole in place then drilled three holes, attaching the 4x4 to the ceiling/floor joist with carriage bolts about three feet from the back wall of the house. Next, she nailed two 2x4's to the base of the pole and attached the other ends to the framing against the basement wall. She gave the scratching pole a tug. It seemed to be firmly in place so she gave it a couple of serious pushes with her foot. It didn't budge.

"What do you think Misty?" she asked. The cat just watched from her perch on top of some boxes filled with Christmas and other seasonal decorations.

Jane went over and picked Misty up and carried her to the pole, setting her on the floor. She made some scratching movement with her own hands, but Misty just watched. Jane took Misty's front paws, stretched them up the pole and pressed on the toe pads to extend the claws, placing them into the fabric. The cat was fully extended and got the hint right away, pulling her claws through the material.

While Misty played with the pole Jane took a skein of yarn from one of her shopping bags and wound it up into a tight ball, securing the end inside.

"Misty, here try this," tossing the ball of yarn toward her.

The cat took off after the ball immediately and began to play with it hitting it from one corner to another, chasing it around, batting it with her paws. She was totally engulfed with the toy for fifteen minutes while Jane finished cleaning up the sawdust and put the tools away.

2

Buck pulled into a parking space at Townsend Aviation and grabbed his flight bag from the back seat of his Explorer.

"Hi Buck," Bull Townsend greeted him as he walked in. Bull was a big, burly black man who had been one of the original Tuskegee Airmen. Buck figured he had to be in his eighties, but he still came to work everyday and he still gave flying lessons.

"Hi Bull, how have you been?"

"Oh, not bad for an old guy. Rose is having a lot of problems though. The Alzheimer's is getting worse. It's hard leaving her at home alone now. I was on my way home one day last week and she was walking down the street about half a mile from home. I picked her up and asked her where she was going and she said she was walking over to Charles' house, he's one of our sons. Only problem is he lives in Atlanta. I'm either going to have to quit working to stay home and take care of her or put her into a memory care center where they have the place all locked up so they can't wander off. I've tried having someone come in while I'm at work three different times, but they just didn't work out."

"That's very sad."

"Yeah, I don't like any of the choices at this point." Bull stated. "You get 115Q again today."

"Hi Bull," Marie said as she walked in the door.

"Hi Marie, how have you been?"

"Great, it's a beautiful day for a flight," Marie responded excitedly.

"It's CAVU to the moon," clear and visibility unlimited, Bull said. "It should be a spectacular day to fly around the islands."

"That's where we're headed," Buck stated. "See you in a couple hours.

Buck and Marie headed out to the aircraft and he began the preflight while Marie got comfortable in the aircraft. After pogoing the fuel, checking the wings, flaps, tires and engine compartment he untied the aircraft and belted in.

He took out the checklist, checked the yoke, flaps and he opened the side window, yelled outside, "clear" and cranked the engine over. After giving it a few seconds to warm up he let the breaks go and then checked them.

Buck called ground for taxi instructions with information Bravo, weather information, and was cleared to the active runway via taxiway golf. After the run-up check he was cleared for takeoff.

Buck taxied over and turned onto the active runway, stopped, and ran the engine up to full power and let the breaks off. At sixty knots he pulled the

yoke back and the aircraft began to
climb.

Fifteen minutes later they could see the
islands of the north Puget Sound off in
the distance; Orcas, Lucas, Camano and
many other smaller islands. They leveled
off at five thousand feet.

"Hey, look down there, there's
something in the water. It looks like a
pod of whales!" Marie exclaimed, as she
pointed off to the right of the plane.

Buck banked the aircraft to the right
and began descending. "Pretty cool, there
must be eight to ten of them."

"Oh how exciting," Marie said,
relaxing a little more. She knew Buck
loved to fly, but she wasn't all that
relaxed in the little aircraft, even
though she knew Buck was a very competent
pilot with over five thousand hours of
flight time.

After watching the whales for over
half an hour they flew over a few of the
islands. Then Buck turned the aircraft to
the east and climbed back toward
Arlington field.

"Arlington this is Cessna 115 Quebec
twenty miles north west at five thousand
feet, inbound for a full stop,
information Charlie."

"Cessna 115 Quebec this is Arlington
Field, roger you are cleared to the
initial runway 35, report inbound."

"Arlington this is Cessna 115 Quebec
cleared to the initial runway 35, report
inbound."

Buck was descending inbound, made the turn at the initial and reported. He headed straight for the numbers, then flared it out just before touching down, making a smooth landing.

"That was an air force pilot's landing. You usually put it down right on the numbers," Marie said.

"I've been working on it. I know you don't like the hard landings, but twenty years of landing on aircraft carriers you hit the numbers or you get to go around and do it again. That doesn't make for good landing grades," Buck explained, "I'm not getting graded now, and it isn't so critical. There's plenty of runway here."

Inside Townsend Aviation they chatted with Bull for a few minutes and headed to the parking lot.

"I need to get something to eat before going back to work," Marie said, "I'm starving."

"Let's go to the Small Café, it's only about five minutes away. It's where Eric and I used to go when I was teaching him to fly. The food's great there. In fact, I think the soup special on Wednesday is usually Spotted Owl soup. It's really good."

"Isn't that illegal to make soup out of spotted owls?"

"I think it's really chicken soup, but the loggers love it. The place is usually packed on Wednesday, although it's past the prime lunch hour crowd time now.

Follow me," Buck said, giving Marie a kiss and closing her car door.

When they walked into the Small Café Ranger Rick Dance stood up and waved to them. "Buck over here."

"It's Rick Dance," he said to Marie. "Mind if we eat with him?" he asked Marie.

"Not at all, you haven't seen him for a long time."

Buck introduced Marie to Rick and they sat down and ordered the specialty 'spotted owl' soup and sandwiches.

"How's the cougar studies going?" Buck asked.

"One of my study cats, a female, was hit by a car last week. I'd been following her for about four years. It was a tough break. When I started out I collared thirty cats during a period of about a year and a half. I finished collaring them four years ago. I'm down to twenty now. Two others were hit by cars. Two had to be put down by the fish and wildlife enforcement officers for depredation and three were shot by hunters. The other two just disappeared. Collars may have stopped working. Maybe shot by hunters and they buried or dismantled the collar. No way to know really. The batteries may have just gone dead."

"I've been studying cougars some myself since Eric and I went cougar hunting a few years ago," Buck said.

"Really, maybe you'd like to go with me after lunch. I have to put a new collar on a cat that's not very far from here. I'm replacing the collars with some newer high tech ones that have better transmitters and the batteries seem to last a lot longer."

Buck looked over at Marie, questioningly. "You might as well go with him. I think the experience would be good for your cougar research too. You don't have anything else to do this afternoon do you?" Marie asked.

"No, actually my afternoon is completely free. Sure, Id like to go along, sounds like it might be fun. Some first hand experience with cougars would round out my research into attacks on humans. Maybe I'll learn a little more about them," Buck said.

Buck paid for all the meals and Rick thanked him for the lunch as they exited the café.

"Probably easier if we both go in my SUV," Rick stated. "It may get a little rough going getting in there. It's pretty much on the way going back home after we're done to drop you off back here."

"Fine by me," Buck said, giving Marie a kiss goodbye. "See you at home tonight."

"Okay, I'll probably have to work a little late tonight for taking such a long lunch. Should be home by seven though," Marie said.

"I'll bring home a pizza then." They waved as they each went their way.

"So tell me about this cougar we're going after," Buck asked.

"It's a female, a little over three years old. Good health, about one hundred pounds. We'll weigh her and check out her teeth and general condition when we put the new collar on her."

"So does she just lay down and wait for you when she sees you coming?" Buck quipped

Rick laughed, "Not quite that easy. But she is one of the easiest one's I have. She usually hisses and snarls a little when she sees me coming, but it's never tried to run away from me like many of them do. We should be able to get her with one tranquilizer shot. They're not all as easy as her. Most of my study animals I have to chase for awhile till they get tired, or I take hounds with me to tree them. I've got one really aggressive male, about seven years old. He's a big one too. I always take another biologist with me when I have to work with him. I'm always holding a forty-five, when my partner uses the tranq gun. I've nearly had to shoot him a couple times. It takes a little time for the sedative to take effect with him. He usually comes down out of the tree pretty fast after he's been hit. Which way he's going is a mystery, but he's so aggressive he might attack just for fun."

"I went out on a call with a fish and game enforcement officer call about six months ago. A rancher had twelve sheep killed one night. The ranch was in that cougar's known area so I assume it was him. He's mean like that. The fish and game officer got hounds out there, but they never did find him or any other cougar. It was clear that it was done by a cougar though. I never told the fish and game officers it was probably my cat. He's never done anything like this before so I'll keep a close eye on him. If anything like that ever happens in his area again I may need to move him."

"Why would it kill so many sheep at once? It can't possibly think that it could eat that much," Buck asked.

"Oh it happens more than you'd guess with cougars. I've seen deer, even cattle that have been killed by cougars and they never ate any of it. Near as I can tell some cougars just kill for the fun of the chase."

"Probably don't want to tell the animal rights activists about that. They don't like anyone dispelling their theories that cougars only kill what they have to eat to survive. They've made up their minds, don't confuse them with the facts," Buck responded.

They were about thirty miles away from the café and turned off the main road onto a dirt road immediately adjacent to a new, high density housing development. Rick stopped the SUV and took out the hand held GPS positioning device. He punched in a few numbers and waited for the response. The computer queried the system for her collar ID.

The needle swung, indicating a line of bearing and a distance to the target's location. "Okay, we've got her. Looks like she's right about the same place as usual. She's got a good food source here so she doesn't get that far away."

They paralleled the housing development for about ten minutes until they came to a stand of trees on a small hill. The dirt road they had been following came to an end at the edge of the tree line. Rick stopped the car.

"We'll need to walk in from here, but it probably isn't going to take that long to get there," Rick said and climbed out of the SUV.

Buck got out his side and Rick opened the back door, taking out a backpack and the tranquilizer gun.

"This way," Rick nodded to his left and headed to an animal trail that led into the woods.

"This looks like it used to be a well used trail, but it's little overgrown," Buck observed.

"Yeah, she's been around this area for about a year now. I collared her as a kitten when she was still with her mother. That was about ten miles from here. She was dispersed when she was sixteen months old. When she first got here there were a lot of deer around. I've seen very few signs of deer lately. I imagine she's eaten most of them. I've been expecting her to move out of this area, hopefully back into the mountains where she can feed on deer. That's more normal for cougar. But, either she's getting enough here or the bordering areas have cougars that are not friendly and she can't find another place to home range. If that's the case and she runs out of cats and dogs here, she will move into another housing area."

They made their way to the top of a ridge and Rick stopped, holding out the GPS system he punched a few numbers in. It quickly gave a bearing and distance to the contact. He took out his binoculars and scanned in the direction the GPS indicated.

"She's over there," Rick said, pointing to the southeast. About a hundred yards, up in the tree," he handed the binoculars to Buck.

After a few minutes Buck said, "Oh yeah, I see her. She's really well camouflaged. That's amazing you can find her so easy."

"It didn't used to be this easy. Before we got this GPS tracking system it could easily take days to locate one cat. We had to use hounds to find them back then too. The hounds put a lot of stress on the cats."

Buck looked past the cat at the housing development. "She's only about two hundred yards from those houses. That seems kind of dangerous."

"Yes, it's kind of ironic," Rick explained. "She goes into the housing development almost every night, looking for cats and dogs. Probably gets an occasional raccoon or possum too. I've done a few one minute position recordings on her at night. She just weaves her way through the houses, hunting."

"That sounds mighty unsafe to the people that live there to me," Buck said.

"Nothing has happened yet. She's pretty non-aggressive. If it was some of the other cats I'm studying I would have moved her a long time ago."

"You know, I've been studying cougar for a few years now. Have you ever studied cougar attacks on humans?"

"Nope, never have," Rick simply stated.

"Well, I have. There are a few things that some of the attacks have in common. In some of the attacks on humans the cougars had been living around humans and eating domestic cats and dogs for some time before they attacked the human," Buck said.

"I wouldn't know about that. All I know is that attacks on humans are very rare. Let's crouch down and sneak up on her," Rick said.

They moved slowly at the edge of the foliage line. About twenty yards away she got sight of them and hissed.

"She's got us now," Rick said and stood up, advancing toward her.

When she saw Buck she became agitated, standing up on the branch, hissing loudly.

"I thought you said she was real laid back," Buck asked.

"She usually is, but she's used to me being alone. Good news is she's giving me a much bigger target by standing up. Usually she just lays on the branch, only hissing a little," Rick said as he inserted the dart in the rifle.

"Okay hon, this will only hurt for a second."

Rick laid the barrel of the rifle in the crook of a tree branch, aiming. He took his time waiting for the right moment. A missed shot with the tranquilizer gun was expensive. She gradually began to settle down and relax. He wanted to get her while she was still standing, before she got real relaxed and laid back down on the branch. 'Pop', the air rifle sent the dart into the side of her front right leg just below the shoulder.

She hissed, and stood steady for about five seconds. Gradually she began to sag and grabbed her left front claws into the tree trunk, slowly descending, grabbing the trunk every few feet. About ten feet from the ground the effect of the sedative increased and she lost her grip, falling the rest of the way to the ground. She took a stumbling step and fell. Making an attempt to get up again, she collapsed and went out cold.

"That went really well. She knows what to expect and she's usually not a problem. Some of the others jump out of the tree to run, and they can get out of sight on the ground when the sedative takes effect. They don't usually get too far though. Others fight it, stay up high in the tree until they're really sedated and fall all the way to the ground. Much higher chance of one getting seriously hurt that way. Fortunately, I haven't had to take any to the vet yet. They fall thirty feet sometimes, hitting branches along the way and don't sustain any serious injuries."

They each kneeled down beside her. Buck stroked his hand over her head and down her back. "Just like a big house cat."

Moving quickly Rick pulled her eyelids back and checked her eyes with a flashlight. Then he opened her mouth and checked her teeth. "Teeth and mouth look good."

Rick pulled a canvas blanket out of his backpack and spread it out. Buck helped him move the cat onto the canvas. They rigged the weight scale to the canvas, threw a rope over a tree limb, and lifted her up.

"One hundred and one pounds. Same as last time." He logged it into his notebook.

Rick put on disposable gloves and handed a pair to Buck. Next he ran his hands along the full length of the cat on both sides, feeling for injuries or sores. Then he checked her paws and claws. He pried her mouth open and placed a rubber wedge between the teeth so he could examine her mouth easier. He moved the lips around to get a good look at her teeth, tongue, gums and the general condition of the inside of her mouth.

Buck did some examination on his own, taking in her size. He examined the paws.

"Big paws," he observed. "Powerful animal, not much fat either," as he felt the leg muscles.

"Yes, they are powerful animals. She looks pretty healthy. Let's get her a new collar." He started unscrewing the in-place collar while Buck got the new one

out of the backpack and removed it from
the container. As Rick was tightening
down the new collar the cat stirred
slightly.

"Whoops," Rick said. "We better make
this quick," tightening it down. She
stirred again.

"Okay, it's time for us to get out of
here, now," Rick said jumping back. Buck
started to grab the backpack. "Leave it
all there. We'll come back and get it.
She may not be in a good mood when she
comes out of it, and they can come out of
it real fast sometimes."

They ran back to the cover of some
brush and hid in the bushes just as she
stood up. The cat looked around, then
walked off to the south, not looking
back.

"She didn't seem to be drowsy at all."
Buck noted.

"It happens that way sometimes. That's
why we beat a hasty retreat. Using
sedatives is always guesswork. I know
from history she doesn't usually need a
lot. But, she may have had more adrenalin
in her because of you being here. It's
hard to tell. Sometimes you can shoot one
three or four times, what would usually
seem like a lethal dose, and they don't
even seem to be affected. The big ones
are a lot more unpredictable.

After she was out of sight they
returned and put all the equipment back
into the backpack.

On the way back to the truck Buck
said, "That was very interesting. It was
amazing to see a live one up close, even

touch it, pretty awesome. I'm still thinking that it isn't safe for it to be living that close to a housing development though."

"I've been studying cougars for a long time. This situation is not really that unusual. I talk to other researchers at conventions and have some contacts I've developed over the years. E-mail's a great way to stay in touch and keep each other up on the latest developments. There are cougars living close to people and developments all over the west. Didn't happen fifteen or twenty years ago, but it's been going on for at least ten years now. There's only been about four cougar attacks on humans per year for the last twenty years or so. That's not very many. And none of them have been by cougars that are living next to people."

"What about the one in California? A cougar killed the mountain biker and then attacked another woman mountain biker in the same area not long after the first attack."

"Well, that's the one exception. Most of the incidents happen in more remote areas where you might expect a cougar to be."

"So if this didn't happen fifteen years ago, why do you think it's happening today?" Buck asked.

"No clue. It's curious for sure, but they just seem to be adapting to being around people. For my money they can eat all the stray cats and dogs they want. There are a lot of people who let their dogs out to run free at night. Sometimes those dogs pack together. That can be dangerous too. The cougars are doing us a favor when they can eat those dogs, as far as I'm concerned anyway."

On the way back to the Small Café to retrieve Buck's SUV he couldn't help thinking about the cougar's proximity to the housing development. He could understand Rick's desire to protect the animals because he'd been studying them for years. However, it seemed to him that public safety was a more important issue here. It was also curious, he thought, that Rick said it was happening all over the west. If this was a behavioral change that was happening in a lot of areas there must be a reason for it. It would seem that there were the two possible logical conclusions. One, the cougar population was growing and they had no place else to go, since they are so highly territorial. Two, they followed their primary food source, deer, like predatory animals have done forever, right into the housing developments where deer had been thriving for the last fifteen years.

At the Small Café Buck said, "Thanks for taking me with you. That was quite an experience."

"Thanks for coming along. It's nice have some company once in a while."

They said farewell and each headed off in his own direction.

Buck stopped and picked up a family size chicken garlic pizza at Papa Murphy's on the way home for dinner. When he heard the garage door going up, signaling Marie's arrival, he popped it in the oven.

"Hi honey, I'm home," Marie announced as she came through the door from the garage into the kitchen.

"Hi Marie," giving her a quick kiss on the cheek, Buck said. "The pizza should be ready in about ten minutes."

"Bob, Wendy, mom's home, time for dinner," he yelled up the stairs.

"Okay, I'm starving. I'll be right down."

When Wendy arrived Buck asked, "Can you set the table for us?"

"Sure," she responded.

"Where's Bob?" Buck asked.

"He went down into the canyon to do some research for his school project. He said not to wait for him for dinner," Wendy replied.

"How did your cougar excursion with Rick go?" Marie asked.

"It went real smooth. We found the female cougar in no time at all with his GPS system. It's really slick. She went down with one tranquilizer shot and just kind of slid out of the tree. She started coming out of it while Rick was screwing down the new collar. That created some excitement when we had to get out of there in a hurry. I could have actually spent quite a bit more time with her. We had to leave our stuff there and go back after it after she left."

"Oh, I bet that was exciting," Wendy said.

"It wasn't too bad. She gave us some warning that the tranquilizer was wearing off, so we high tailed it for the bushes. The cougar just got up and walked off."

"Cool," Wendy said. "How big was it?"

"It was a three year old female. She weighed a hundred and one pounds. The interesting thing was that she was living immediately adjacent to a new housing development. The tree she was in when we found her was only about two hundred yards from the backyards."

"That doesn't sound good," Marie said.

"My thoughts too, but Rick said it's not all that uncommon in the west. He stays in touch with other researchers."

"Wow, that's interesting." Marie responded, finishing off her last bite of pizza.

Bob walked in the door and laid his backpack on the kitchen floor. "What's for dinner?"

"Pizza, if you hurry, dad's about to finish it off," Marie said.

"How's the project going?" Buck asked.

"It's pretty interesting," Bob said. "I never knew there was such a variety of wildlife right in our backyard."

"Find anything really unusual?" Wendy asked.

Bob pondered how to answer. "Nothing too earth shaking," he returned.

3

Jane had been laid off from her job. The stock of the company she worked for had taken a nose dive after a series of unimpressive earnings reports. Many other biotech companies like hers were also hard hit. It had been her first job after receiving a Bachelors degree. What an incredible stroke of luck, to get in at the bottom floor at the new technology upstart. Like many of her co-workers she had nearly a million dollars in stock at the top of the market. It was an unheard of amount of money for someone who had only been out of college for a scant four years.

Her parents, who were in their early fifties, had almost nothing in the bank. They'd been farmers all their lives and it was a tough life. They were having trouble now too. Fiercely independent, she would only consider moving back in with them as an extreme last resort.

She had hung on to the stock for the long term, just like the financial people on the business news kept saying on all the investment shows. Stay the course, hold on to the stocks for the long term, the market always comes back. She watched her stock disintegrate like Chinese water torture. In a year and a half her stock was worthless. Six months ago it looked like what little was left of the company would soon fold. The company declared bankruptcy recently and the stock was declared worthless. Even if the company eventually became solvent and issued new stock, the old stock was still worthless. At this point it appeared there was no hope that the company would survive. Their stock had shot up into the stratosphere and with the stock price collapse the company was not able to pay off loans. The company executives had used the employee's retirement fund in a vain attempt to keep the company solvent. The result was that not only did the employees loose their jobs and all their stock value, but they also lost their company sponsored retirement benefits because the executives had used the retirement funds to cover losses.

Jane had valuable knowledge in this new age of technology, but many of the similar companies were in the same situation. She had lost a small fortune in stocks, like many others and was having a hard time finding a new job. By the time her unemployment benefits ran out she had still been unable to find a job using her biotech skills. It didn't take long for her to turn to a survival focus. She became desperate and took a job as a waitress at a restaurant, but business had slowed even there, and it was only part time, three days a week. If she paid her house payment one month, her car payment the next and a credit card payment the next month she might be able to make it until she found a job that paid a livable wage. Working full time at minimum wage paid about half of what was considered to be the federal poverty level. For someone who had been in the top ten percent of the national income bracket, this was a real shock. She tried to be optimistic. She was still young, she figured eventually things would get better. She still had a few thousand dollars in the bank, but it was going fast.

For her now, the pressing problem was Misty. She lay on the sofa next to Jane, her head on her lap. She looked at her and ran her hand over her back. At about one hundred and twenty pounds she was about average size for her age. The problem was that she ate a lot. Jane fed her mostly dry cat food, but on rare occasions she had treated her with raw hamburger. It seemed to whet her appetite. The raw hamburger made her ravenous so she couldn't afford to do it very often. Misty usually would consume a twenty pound bag of cat food every five to seven days. In her financial condition it was difficult to find enough money to feed herself and Misty. She had been a fun and wonderful companion when she was younger. Now, nearly two years later, she was close to coming of age. Occasionally, she would become aggressive for no apparent reason. She had bit her recently during one of these playful times and required antibiotics to cure the infection. Misty had tremendous strength and Jane knew she could tear her apart if she wanted to.

The next day she called the local zoo
and offered to give Misty to them. The
zoo already had a cougar and didn't need
another. She then called a game farm,
same result. There had been consistent
problems with cougars in the northern
Olympic Mountain foothills near numerous
populated areas for the last few years.
The fish and wildlife department
recognized these incidents as a potential
threat to public safety. More
importantly, the potential for
litigation, if someone was killed or
seriously injured by a cougar in an area
that was heavily used for recreational
purposes. That represented a major
potential for financial problems for
state officials. The issue was compounded
by research that indicated that in some
areas cougars had taken up home range
immediately adjacent to densely populated
areas.

The fish and wildlife department had
used dogs to track down and trap or
capture fourteen cougars in the last
year. They gave all of them to a game
farm. Most of them were adult animals and
did not take well to living a captive
life. They were so aggressive that the
game farm had to put all but one to
sleep.

Jane looked at Misty and began to cry.
She just could not put her to sleep. That
night, under the cover of darkness, she
put Misty in the car and drove east on I-
90 past Snoqualmie Ski Resort and took
the first forest service road to the
north. She drove on the paved road,

deeper and deeper into the forest. In about twenty minutes the road turned into a gravel logging road. The forest service was not allowed to sell timber anymore and the road had deteriorated. She put it in four wheel drive, but soon decided to stop because of the darkness. Fortunately, there was enough room and she turned around. She opened her door and stepped out. Misty was eager and jumped out right behind her. She was not used to being out in the woods at night, but she seemed to like it.

Jane put her foot on the front bumper and climbed up, sitting on the left side of the hood. She watched as Misty roamed around in the dim light of the moon, disappearing and then re-appearing. After twenty minutes Misty jumped up on the hood and lay down, her head near Jane. The warmth of the engine beneath her, she began to purr. Jane stroked the back of her head, a tear rolled down her cheek. Misty lifted her head and laid it on Jane's leg, looking up at her. She seemed to be saying, 'What's wrong?' This only made it worse. She began to sob uncontrollably.

In a few minutes a noise came from the edge of the woods. It was too dark to see what it was, but something was moving through the underbrush not far away. Misty picked her head up and suddenly became intensely interested. She jumped off the hood and slowly began moving toward the noise, crouching down low, stopping every few seconds to get a better focus on the sound. She slowly moved out of Jane's visibility into the darkness of the forest. She could still hear the animal moving in the brush. In about ten minutes there was a sound of rapid movement in the woods and then a short, sharp squeal, followed by silence.

Jane took this fortuitous incident as an omen that Misty would be able to make it on her own. She got into the car and unhurriedly drove away. If Misty was able to catch prey she could survive and Jane felt better about leaving her there. On the drive back home she didn't feel great about what she had done, but felt that it was the right thing to do.

Six weeks later Jane was stretched out on the sofa in her living room watching the television. The ten o'clock news was on and she was beginning to doze off. The drapes were open across the sliding glass door leading to the patio and the backyard. Misty's cat toys, albeit big cat toys, were still strewn around the house.

Almost asleep, Jane sensed a slight clicking sound. The noise was consistent, but not sequentially repetitive. She focused on the sound as she began to be more awake. It didn't seem to be coming from the TV. She looked over at the sliding glass door, and there was Misty, pawing at the glass door with her claws.

Jane jumped up and ran to the door flinging it open. Misty jumped in and stood up on her hind legs, placing her paws on Jane's shoulders and began gently licking the side of Jane's neck. Jane wrapped her arms around the back of the big cat and hugged Misty.

After five minutes in the embrace Jane said, "I'll bet you're hungry, come on." She led the way to the pantry and pulled out what remained of the twenty pound bucket of cat food, scooping out a big portion and poured it into the cat bowl, which lay undisturbed on the laundry room floor. Misty quickly finished off the bowl and Jane re-filled it.

Jane stood watching Misty pensively, apparently she had not been able to find as much to eat as she had originally thought. She appeared to be quite a bit thinner than she used to be, but she did not appear to be unhealthy. How on earth had she found her way back here? After the third bowl Misty was finally sated. They strolled together back to the living room and Jane stretched out again on the sofa. Misty stepped up onto the sofa and lay down, head on Jane's chest. Jane stroked her head and neck, wondering what to do next. She had always been a strong believer in fate. Perhaps this was a sign that she should not have set her free.

Misty began to purr loudly and Jane relaxed, slowly fading off into a dream. She was walking in the woods, close to the ground. She roamed the night, looking through a cougar's eyes, seeing in black and white. Seeking the night creatures of the forest; raccoons, possum, rabbits, moving slowly, stopping to listen, stalking, missing her kill, hungry.

Then there was a loud, repetitive noise. When she realized the irritating sound was the phone ringing, she looked over at the clock, nine fifteen.

"Wow, I haven't slept this late in a long time." She was too late to catch the phone. She picked up the handset and checked the caller ID. From the number it looked like one of those irritating, invasive sales calls. She went to the laundry room and poured a large helping of dry cat food into Misty's bowl. Upstairs she showered and then went outside to work in the garden. She wanted to think out this new turn of events. She had finally gotten over Misty being set free and now she was back. 'Now what?' she thought to herself.

In the laundry room Buck Logan snapped the lead onto his dog Scout's collar and stepped out the door into the garage. He pressed the garage door opener and headed down the driveway. Taking a right at the mailbox, they walked along Cedar Lane until they intercepted the natural trail at the end of the street. Scout sniffed at the tree trunks on the way leaving a little of his own scent at each interesting site to attract the curiosity of the next dog that passed along the trail. It was just before noon and the trail was deserted. Thirty minutes later they exited the trail a quarter mile from home to make the trip complete without having to pass back through the same way they had previously traveled.

The first house off the trail was a fairly new one story house with a daylight basement. It had a nicely kept flower garden and the lawn was recently mowed. It stood out because most of the houses in the neighborhood were two stories. In the front yard was a woman, probably in her late twenties working in the flower bed. The scene caught Buck's attention immediately because directly above the woman, watching her through the window was a cougar. It seemed completely at peace and content to observe the woman.

"Hello there," Buck said. "You know there's a cougar in your window?"

"Oh hi, that's Misty," the woman said, standing up. Jane thought she had left Misty in the basement, where she usually was when Jane was not in the house. She must have left the door ajar.

"That's not a sight one sees very often." Scout noticed the big cat and moved closer to Buck pressing up against his leg. Scout was a Dalmatian who was a very dedicated family dog, but could be aggressive to strangers, especially when they came to the door or onto their property. The cougar was watching the dog intently.

The woman walked over to the sidewalk. "I'm Jane," she said, extending her hand.

"Buck Logan, nice to meet you. We live over on Cedar Lane."

"I've seen you walking your dog occasionally."

"How old is your cougar?"

"She's about two years old now. I found her shortly after her mother was killed. I raised her from a kitten. She only weighed about ten pounds when I found her."

"She's pretty good sized now. What's she like as a pet?"

"Very gentle and loving, just like a house cat only bigger. She weighs a little over one hundred pounds. About the only difference I can see between her and a house cat is that she eats a lot more. She's pretty strong when she wants to be too."

"Yeah, I'll bet. I don't know if you are aware of this or not, but do you know that it's illegal to have a cougar as a pet in Washington state?"

"No," she said surprised. "I'd never even given it any thought. I don't let her out of the house. I know that wouldn't be wise. I just brought her home when I found her. She would have died if I'd left her out there on her own. She was only a month or so old then. Without a mother to take care of her she wouldn't have stood a chance of surviving."

"The reason I'm telling you is that my next door neighbor's daughter was attacked by a cougar when she got off the school bus a few years ago. She was only five when it happened, but she has the scars to prove it. The neighborhood is still a little skittish over it."

"Yes I imagine so. I know they do attack people occasionally, but Misty is so gentle. I can't believe she would ever attack anyone."

"You never know about animals, even domestic ones will sometimes turn on their owners. Certain types of dogs have a history of aggressive problems. I imagine a cat that size could be a handful if it got mad for some reason."

Agreeing she could only reply, "Yeah." She'd been so happy to see Misty again that she had forgotten about the occasional aggressive behavior Misty had exhibited in the weeks before she took her out to the woods to set her free.

"You could be right." If she got out and attacked someone she would never forgive herself. "Maybe it's time for me to find a proper home for her." She stood there, forced to address the problem again. She contemplated what to do next.

Buck could tell that she was deep in thought. "I've got to get on my way. Nice meeting you Jane."

"Yes, nice meeting you too Buck," she replied absently.

When Buck reached his house he stopped to pick up the mail at the mailbox. Checking the letters on the way up the driveway he sorted out the junk mail. He discarded nine of the ten letters, unopened, in the big, wheeled trash can just inside the garage, pressed the button to close the door and opened the door into the house, ushering Scout in ahead of him. Leaving his shoes at the back door he went to the kitchen, where Scout was standing, waiting patiently. He picked a dog treat from the basket on the counter and looked at Scout, who quickly lay down. Buck tossed her the treat.

"Time for me to get going," Buck said and headed out the door for the outdoor skills classes that he taught at the university.

That night Jane sat on the sofa watching TV. Misty was stretched out on the sofa, just like she did before, head in Jane's lap. Jane stroked her fur. She was calm and content now, but earlier she had become aggressive in a surprise instant that had scared Jane. There had been no provocation at all, but Misty had approached her with her fangs barred and a distant look in her intense yellow eyes. Jane had backed away and tossed Misty a large treat. It distracted Misty and she focused on the treat, then picked it up and walked away to the living room to munch on it.

Jane decided, once again that Misty had to be returned to the wild. How she had found her way back to Jane's house was a mystery. This time she would have to take her farther away.

Early Saturday morning before the sun came up Jane loaded Misty in the back seat of her SUV and blocked her access to the front seat. This way if anyone did look into her car they would not be able to see her. She headed up I-90 and past the Snoqualmie Ski Resort. The last time Jane had set her free in the dark, but she had been a little weary of traveling the back roads in the dark. This time she timed her trip so that the sun was coming up just about the time she exited the I-90 freeway. She took the Kachess Lake exit and drove into the Wenatchee

National Forest wilderness and headed
north into the Cascade Mountains. It was
a steep, winding road that ascended
higher and higher into the mountains.
After passing Kachess Lake she came to a
gravel road. She put the SUV into four
wheel drive and drove for another hour.
Along the way she decided that this was
definitely cougar country.

She had noticed a sign as she passed
the Ski Resort at Snoqualmie. It said the
elevation was 3,500 feet above sea level.
In the two plus hours she had driven
since then she must have climbed another
three thousand feet. There were some
patches of snow to be seen on some of the
higher mountains off in the distance. She
hadn't seen another car, or any other
sign of people since she left I-90.

She pulled out of the road into a
clearing where there was a small meadow
on the lower side of the road. On the
upper side was a steep, densely forested
grade. She opened the door and Misty
sprung out and headed for the meadow. She
raced the full length, then back to the
center of the meadow where she lay down
and rolled in the grass.

Jane watched contentedly as the cat
frolicked in the grass. She was fast,
Jane noted, and powerful.

Suddenly Misty hunkered down in the
grass. She was barely visible, ears
sticking up above the grass line as Misty
crouched down and slowly advanced toward
the tree line.

Jane looked at the tree line in the direction Misty was headed, but did not see the object of her attention.

Suddenly Misty half stood, her tense leg muscles rippled as she sprang forward. Only then did Jane see the deer. Misty landed on its back, jaws clamped down on the back of its neck. Then she did a series of bites on the back of the neck, searching to force the long canine teeth between the vertebrae, to paralyze the deer. When this was not successful Misty reached her right paw around the head and pulled back a rapid jerk. The deer dropped like a stone. This all happened in a few seconds. Since she had not learned this behavior from her mother, it must have been instinctive.

Jane was impressed and awed at the sight of Misty being successful on her own. She was totally focused on the deer and Jane decided this was a good time to depart. She had brought along a five pound sack of cat food hoping it would help Misty adjust to her new surroundings. She deposited the bag on the ground next at the side of the road and opened it up completely at the top. She went back to the SUV and closed the door quietly, trying not to make any noise.

She drove off slowly hoping Misty would not try to follow her. She kept looking in the rear view mirror as she drove away, but there was no indication that Misty was following.

Misty had stayed there for three days, feeding on the deer carcass two to three times a day. Sleeping in a tree nearby where she could see the carcass between feedings. It was cold at night, but in the forties during the day and by the third day the meat was beginning to decay. Since cats won't eat decayed meat, she decided to move on.

She traveled south, in the direction she had come from. Four days later she came to I-90 in the darkness. She'd seen cars and the highway before. She had no compunction about crossing the highway, but it didn't feel right. She headed west, paralleling the freeway for days.

Late one afternoon she awoke feeling different. She climbed down the tree about ten feet from the branch where she had been sleeping. When she had a clear space to the ground she leapt the twenty feet, hitting the ground on the run. She felt full of energy, invigorated. She ran along the stream for an hour in the dying twilight.

That evening, just after dark she found an enormous rock and jumped up on top of it. Stretching out, after running off and on for hours, she was ready for a rest when it hit her. A long, loud guttural scream came up from deep inside her. It caught her by surprise. She had never made that kind of sound before. Then it came again. She felt different. She had urges she had never felt before. She wanted a companion. She lay on the rock, periodically screaming throughout the night. It was a warm, dry evening. Her screams carried for miles.

The mean male listened intently trying to determine the direction, then ran toward the sound. He knew what it meant. He wanted to get there first.

When morning came, the screams stopped. The mean male kept heading in the same direction. Tirelessly, he proceeded at a fast pace all day. When darkness came again, so did the screams. He was closer now, but had to change his direction slightly. As he drew nearer he began to open his mouth, bearing his fangs, exposing the glands that sensed the pheromones emitted in the urine of the female cougar when in heat.

Misty had wandered around in a small area all day, urinating frequently, spraying it to disperse it as widely as possible. She was focused now, intense. She had a mission. As soon as the sun disappeared over the top of the mountains the urge came back and she began screaming again.

Later that evening the mean male sensed the aroma, wafting in the air, very subtlety. It was the smell he was looking for. He got a whiff of the female's urine. He was thirty months old now, in the peak of his early adult development. He had been expressing semen for weeks. When his glands got a full whiff of the pheromones in the urine he crouched down and shot a stream of semen three feet. He let out a brief hiss, in an attempt to get the female to disclose her position.

She had been screaming regularly an hour ago, but she had been quiet for the last twenty minutes. He went around a bend and came across two cougars, one sitting down, the other slowly circling her, opening his jaws to take in the aroma of the pheromones. The still one saw him right away, the other re-focused his attention. It was a good thirty pounds bigger than he. The male immediately left the female and moved toward him, head up, he was focused for battle. Hoping his size would intimidate the interloper and scare him off, the first suitor hissed when he got within ten feet of the mean male.

The mean male however, knew exactly what he wanted. He sprang without warning, catching the other male at the base of the neck in his jaws. He had a vice grip bite right where the neck met the upper shoulder.

A night piercing scream echoed through the woods. Blood flew, as the two twisted, claws reaching for any possible purchase. The bigger cougar continued to scream so loud that it could be heard for miles. The mean male clamped down even more with his jaws, and dug his claws into the side of his opponent. The bigger cougar was unable to dislodge the opponent's powerful bite. It was in an awkward position to get a grip on the other. They rolled around on the ground, the bigger cat continuing to scream, twisting, trying to shake the other off.

The twisting action swung the mean male like a pendulum, creating great force as he clung to the neck. The force of his weight dislodged the mean male, taking with him a chunk from the other male's throat, along with it the jugular vein was ripped open. Blood sailed in every direction as the other male came back, catching the mean male in the right flank he sunk his claws into his back. His intense agitation and forceful movements pumped the blood out of the severed jugular vein in spurts. Before he could rip a chunk out of the flank he lost his grip and fell to the ground. He stood back up and tried to make another assault, but he had lost too much blood from the severed jugular vein.

The mean male swung around quickly and seized the opponent in his jaws at the back of the neck, lifted him off the ground and swung him around like a rag doll. The opponent's strength sapped away from the loss of blood, his muscles slowly giving way. The mean male took advantage of his upper hand and broke the opponent's neck with a powerful twist of his head. The opponent went limp, signaling victory. He quickly lost interest in the fight and turned his attention to the female.

He circled her a few times, sniffing with his fangs barred, then rubbed his head on her neck, nuzzling her. She hissed a gentle hiss. She crouched down and he mounted her. They mated throughout the night, taking cat naps between sessions. Even though he had not eaten for days, he had no interest in eating.

The next day they began to consume the dead male cougar, between mating sessions. Three days later Misty felt that her mission was completed, but the male was not ready to leave. Whenever she tried to chase him away he grabbed her by the neck and mated again.

That night when he was asleep she took off and headed down the mountain. She followed the stream at the base of the mountain as it worked its way downhill.

4

Bob Logan was a senior in high school. He was young for a senior. He had started kindergarten early when he was only four years and nine months old, against the advice of the school principal. He had seemed to Buck and Marie to be well ahead of his peers so they decided to go ahead and register him. If a problem developed they could always keep him back a year. If he was going to experience difficulties keeping up in class the problems would become apparent within the first year. It would not be a problem or present a stigma for him if they had to keep him back at that age, like it would in later years.

It was the beginning of the school year. He was on the school swimming and diving team during the winter trimester and pole vaulted on the track team in the spring, but he did not go out for a sport in the first, the fall tri, of the year. Mainly because none of the sports that were offered; football, cross country or tennis, interested him. He had nearly qualified for the state diving championships last year and had made the height to go to state championships in

track near the end of the season last
year. Unfortunately, he sprained his
ankle during practice the day before the
district track meet. He'd vaulted at the
district meet, in spite of the pain, but
was only able to make fourteen feet five
inches, one inch short of the requirement
to advance on to the state meet.

The bell rang signaling the end of
Bob's biology class, his last class of
the day. He left the classroom shortly
after the two thirty-five bell and went
to his locker, dropping off his biology
book and picking up his calculus book to
do his homework for the night. He was in
no hurry to depart the school grounds.
Taking his time would decrease the
potential for any of his friends to see
him walking home.

Buck, Bob's father, had recently
suspended his driving privileges. Last
week Bob had made a trip to the local
grocery store for a quick lunch, but
lunch period was short and he was running
late. To top it off Bob was driving
grandma's old car, which they had
inherited when Buck's mother passed away
from cancer. He didn't drive Old Betsy
very often. It had an especially long
hood, which he was not accustomed to, and
it caused a miscalculation of space and
distance as he pulled into the parking
space on his hasty return to school.

Bob got out of the car and studied the
damage. Old Betsy, had sustained no
damage at all. The downside was the
parked car. It had a medium sized dent in
the rear driver's side quarter panel. He

went to the school administration main office to report the incident. Some high school students would have left the scene and parked somewhere else, shirking the responsibility of the incident. Not Bob, that was not the way he was brought up. Accept responsibility for one's actions even if the result was not pleasant.

He met the owner after school. She was nearly in tears when he arrived.

"It was my first day to drive the car," Katie said. "It's a brand new car. Today is the first time I've driven it to school. It was a present from my dad for one year of accident and ticket free driving," she lamented.

The result was a small crease in the rear panel of Katie's new car. Bob knew that this was going to be an expensive mistake. He had already discovered, from his friends auto accidents, that car repairs, even the smallest dent repair, was outrageously overpriced.

Bob felt bad about the incident, "I'm really sorry Katie. It was totally my fault." Bob had only been driving for one week. He reflected on the tickets his older brother, Eric, had gotten in the early months of his driving experience. It seemed to be a normal part of the process to him. A setback, to be sure, but he was not about to say anything to his friends at school about why he was not driving. Time would pass and it would be history and no one would be the wiser. But, for high school students the perception of how their peers see them was paramount to them. Just keep a low profile, be quiet about it, and no one would notice.

He hung around the commons area until three, when most of the students had departed, then walked out the main doors and headed through the parking lot. He'd walk home today, no way would he take the bus and let everyone know that he had lost his driving privileges already after only one week of driving.

"Hi Bob, want a ride home?" Anne, the cute young sophomore asked.

"Hi Anne, no thanks. I need the exercise." He kind of liked her, but didn't want her to know of his plight. He waved as she drove off.

Walking past the parking lot toward the watershed he was deep in thought about his biology assignment for the trimester. He had to do a paper after each trimester, but he also had to do an oral presentation about his project to the class each time.

Bob descended the trail that led down to the bottom of the watershed where it intersected the main trail. He headed east as the trail wandered its way along side a stream that flowed down from the mountains, eventually flowing into the Snoqualmie River. The river flowed down hill through spectacular falls until it eventually poured its contents into the Puget Sound.

It was a picturesque setting surrounded by beautiful evergreen trees, salal, Oregon grape and wild berries. Occasionally, a tree squirrel chattered in the evergreen trees above the trail.

The blue jays chased each other from tree to tree, squawking.

Bob figured he'd study biology in college and was now taking a biology class that was actually three classes back to back for his whole senior year. The special course was for advance placement students. The students were to undertake a project for the class. It was just the beginning of the school year, but he had yet to decide what the project would be about.

It was a little less than two miles from the school grounds to his house through the watershed, and the trail went right through the area behind his house. It would save him about fifteen minutes of walking time to get home if he walked steadily and it was usually an interesting walk along the stream. The problem was that there were so many interesting things to see, now that he was taking biology, that it actually took him longer to go through the canyon. He had spent uncountable hours in the canyon before, but now he saw it in a different way. Few of his fellow students who walked home, instead of taking the bus, took the watershed route. Most preferred to walk with friends along the sidewalk, occasionally stopping at the Quick Mart for a soda or candy bar along the way. Bob wasn't in a social mood today and preferred to be by himself.

The watershed had been created naturally through years of water runoff in the wet winters of the northwest. It was actually a very pleasant place for a walk. There were lots of trees and foliage and occasionally he would see a deer along the way. Sort of like taking a walk in the country woods, only it was surrounded by houses.

As he walked along the trail next to the stream he paid more attention to the flow of the water than he did to the trail. The stream was about ten feet across and varied in depth from a few inches to sometimes more than two feet deep. Occasionally when it was raining hard the stream would swell and engulf much of the trail. About half way home he noticed something in the water that looked out of place. He stopped and laid down his pack to take a closer look. Sitting back on his heels he studied the sphere. It was slightly larger than a golf ball, but it looked like a mass of gelatin, all lumpy and bumpy. He picked up a stick and began to probe the ball. It moved around freely, but was rather heavy. He wondered what it was. After about half an hour of studying it and the other contents of the little pool, he hoisted his pack and resumed his trek, he was in no hurry. Along the way he thought about his biology assignment and what he might select as a project.

At the dinner table that night Bob said, "I have to do a project for my biology class. It's supposed to last for the whole year, since it's actually a three tri-mester long class for accelerated students, I'm not sure what I want to do it on."

"Well, since it's biology, how about a nature theme," Buck responded.

"There's some great nature trails right out back," Marie added.

"Yeah, I know I took the canyon trail home from school today." Then it hit him. "I know, I'll do a bio-diversity theme. There's all kinds of life right there in the canyon. It's really kind of cool to have all the wildlife right in the backyard, even though this is more like living in the city now."

"That's a neat idea," Wendy said. "Maybe I can help you? It sounds like fun."

Bob wasn't too keen on having his little sister tag along but he didn't want to sound like the ungrateful big brother, "Yeah, maybe."

The next day when the final bell rang Bob was excited about his walk home through the canyon. He wasted no time gathering his homework assignments and headed for the trail. At the bottom of the canyon he began looking around even more closely today than yesterday. He thought the answer to his biology assignment was in the canyon, probably in the stream, but what was it going to be?

The walk home through the canyon took about thirty minutes if he walked at a steady pace without stopping. It took him over an hour yesterday. Today he wasn't in any hurry and took time to observe the different things in the watershed. He let his mind wander about what he could focus on for his project.

He sat down on a rock and laid his pack on the ground. Looking at the flow of water in the stream, then the trees and the brush, which was actually a variety of different kinds of plants. He figured he would need to do some studying to find out what the plants were, and which ones were edible. They probably provided food for some of the animals that lived in the watershed. The trees too, maybe some of them were actually fruit trees, and, of course, the stream. It was the life blood of the canyon. Without water nothing could live there. He knew from playing in the canyon with Eric and his other friends when he was younger that the water flow decreased substantially in July and August when there was very little, if any, rain. But, even then there was always some water flowing. That would mean there could be fish or other life that depended on being in the water at all times.

He got up and walked further up the canyon toward home and found the pool where he had seen the sphere the day before. Laying down his pack he picked up a stick and searched around, probing with the stick until he found the gelatinous glob again. He poked at the ball. It seemed to be a little larger today. It also looked a little different. There were little tiny black specks in it. Then, out of the corner of his eye he saw something rather small move. Focusing on it he realized it was a fish.

The pond was large enough that the water was barely moving. The fish was bobbing back and forth toward the surface of the water. Then he noticed that it appeared to be eating something that hung just below the surface. He got down so he was looking at the surface at a flat angle. There were little pinhead sized transparent spots and other things that were moving. The moving things looked like shrimp, about the size of a sesame seed. The tiny fish were feeding on both. Just then he realized it was probably mosquito eggs and mosquito larvae that the fish were eating. 'How cool,' he thought, 'here's nature's way of controlling the mosquito population, a form of checks and balances. It was a natural part of the food chain.' Looking around more he saw other small fish doing the same thing. 'This is amazing,' he thought to himself. 'All the times I've been down here I never took the time to study the really small things that make up this bio-diverse watershed right in my own backyard.'

That night at the table Bob was quiet. He wasn't mad about his license being taken away, he understood that completely. Driving was an exciting step in his life that required him to be responsible in a new way. He was mad at himself for not being more careful and for denting Katie's brand new car. He knew that if he had a new car and someone else had hit it, he'd be pissed off. He also realized that having his license taken away had caused him to walk home in the watershed. Perhaps it was fate that had given him his biology project, and he was really excited about that.

After dinner he adjourned to his room to make an outline for his project. He sat at his computer working on his ideas and decided a camera would be a good way to record things for his project. The new digital camera his dad had just purchased was way cool. You could take two hundred high quality pictures on a tiny memory card that was barely bigger than a postage stamp. To top it off the picture quality was quantum leaps better than film pictures. When the picture was put on a computer one could do almost anything one wanted to do with it. The technology was incredible. He could make his whole presentation as a slide show, including short action video clips, on the computer.

He went downstairs. "Hey dad, can I use the new camera for my biology project?"

"Sure, that's pretty much why we got it. New technology creates new ideas. We figured it might have some great potential for school projects and you can shoot as many pictures as you want. It's practically free too, not like the old technology of film pictures. Near as I can see from shooting a couple hundred pictures around here myself the quality is better than film. It's interesting how new technologies make old things obsolete. But some people will cling to the film cameras until they stop making them. People who teach photography will probably be among the last to switch to the new digital technology. Ironically, some teachers are the last people to want to learn something new. Are you coming up with some good ideas for your project?"

"Yeah, I'm going to take pictures of some things I saw in the watershed in the last two days so I can monitor what happens to them. Then I'm going to put it all together on the computer for the presentation."

"Sounds like a plan. I'll be looking forward to seeing how it comes out."

Bob took the camera bag and put the batteries in the charger to make sure they'd be ready for his excursion tomorrow.

The next morning Bob put all the charged batteries back in the camera bag and placed it all in his backpack before breakfast.

"Pancakes?" Buck asked from his desk at the computer without turning around. He was monitoring real time stock prices, but he'd heard Bob come down the stairs. Buck was always at the computer by six each morning, with CNBC on the TV.

Buck turned the stove on to medium and set the pancake grill on the burner. "Feels strange getting you off to school without Eric here."

"Yeah, I kind of miss him."

"I sort of sensed you might. For brothers you two are pretty good pals. That's good, it's the way it should be. He's only a couple of hours away, but when you're in college you've got other priorities. Central Washington University is the only university around the northwest that offers a flight officer program to get a commercial pilot's license. It's a very good program and it's the only thing Eric has ever wanted to do. It's good for him. Next year you'll go off to college and it'll be just mom, Wendy and I then. Have you decided where you want to go yet?"

"Probably to WSU, a lot of my classmates are going there. It's a big school and they offer a lot of different degree choices. Kind of a long way away though."

"Why not UW. It's close, you could probably live at home if you wanted. You've certainly got the grades for it. It's a big name university."

"UW is too big and impersonal. I wouldn't like it there. Besides I think going away to school sounds like more fun."

"Yeah, I can understand that. It does have a big student population. I'm not much for crowds either."

"Morning dad," Wendy said taking a seat at the table.

"Good morning Wendy," Buck said placing two pancakes on her plate. She spread some raspberry jam on the cakes. "How's that jam you and mom made last week out at grandpa's?"

"It's not as good as grandma used to make, but it was our first try at making it without grandma. At least it was her berries and recipe. I miss grandma though. It was fun to make jam with her. She taught me a lot."

"Yes, I miss her too," Buck stated. "I talked to grandpa on the phone last night. He said your jam was good and to tell you and mom that he appreciated you making some for him too."

The sound of a car horn beeped in the driveway. "Thanks for breakfast dad. Burk's giving me a ride to school," Bob said as he grabbed his backpack and headed out the door. As he passed the stairs Marie was coming down to breakfast. "Bye mom."

"Bye Bob, do good in school," giving him a hug before he headed out the door.

"Morning," Marie said, giving Buck a kiss when she came into the kitchen.

Buck handed her a cup of coffee. "The paper's on the table."

She sat down to a plate with a piece of toast on it. "Morning Wendy,"

"Hi Mom, want some of our homemade raspberry jam?"

"Sure, I'll take a little on my toast." After spreading a knife full on her toast she took a bite. "We did a good job. Maybe not quite as good as grandma's, but it's very tasty."

Wendy hastily made a jam sandwich, tossing it into a brown paper bag along with some chips and a small orange juice. "Bye dad," giving him a hug then going over to Marie. "Bye mom" giving her a hug too. "See ya after volleyball practice."

"Bye honey," Buck and Marie said in unison.

"I miss Eric," Marie said, "and next year Bob will be gone too."

"Yeah, me too," lamented Buck, "but that's the way it works. We just have to hope they end up settling somewhere around here after they get out of college. I hope they don't get spread out all over the country after college."

When the final school bell rang Bob was anxious to get to the watershed, but waited in the commons until the parking lot began to clear. He made his way out past the gym and stopped to talk to some friends from the swimming team who were now on the cross country team. When they headed out for their run of the day Bob crossed the parking lot and took the trail down into the canyon.

He went straight to the pool and searched for the gelatinous ball. It was bigger today and the black specks were even more visible. He took out the camera, then grabbed the stick and moved the ball closer, into more shallow water. The black specks appeared to be moving. He was excited and eager to find out what kind of treasure he had found. He sat on the ground and began playing with the camera, adjusting the focus and the zoom to get the best shots. He was totally focused on the pool, trying to get shots of the tiny fish, and maybe even the smaller mosquito larvae too.

The cougar had followed the boy through the watershed, as it had done yesterday. It was monitoring his movement from a closer distance today. The boy came to an open area and the cat stayed behind as the boy continued along the trail and went around the trees and out of sight. The cougar looked around, seeing no other people it ran ahead until it had the boy in its sights again. It watched for a minute, then ran ahead to an ambush spot it was familiar with, knowing the boy would walk right past it within three feet of its concealed site. Hunkering down, the boy appeared to be walking right for the cougar's position.

As the boy neared its tail began to twitch. When he passed the cat observed everything about the boy. His confident walk, the way he swung his arms, his constant steady pace. The boy stopped, set down his pack, then sat on the ground. Slinking down closer to the ground the cat moved in behind a bush only four feet from the boy who sat by a pool of water. It watched intently for ten minutes. Feeling that there was no threat, it slowly crept closer behind the boy until it could nearly touch him.

Suddenly Bob heard a loud whirring sound, just as he felt something touch his back. He spun around. Laying there behind him was a big cougar, purring. He pulled back away from the big cat. His immediate thought was to run, but instinct told him that would not be the thing to do. He remembered the TV documentary on cougar attacks saying not to run if confronted by a cougar. He slowly inched his way backward a little more.

Then suddenly he grasped the reality of the cougar purring. He thought, cats

purred when they were content. The big
cat lay there looking at him, but then
stopped purring as he crept away. Bob
stopped, one part of him said to get
away, but his intuition said the cat was
not a threat. It certainly was not acting
threatening in any way. Bob and his dog,
Scout, were good pals and he felt
comfortable around all animals. Something
drew him back closer to the cat. It lay
there watching until Bob was once again
next to it. He placed his hand gently on
the back of the cougar's head and stroked
it down the cougar's back.

Misty began to purr again. She had
seen this person walk by the house while
she sat in the window seat watching Jane
work in the rose garden. He had even
stopped to talk with Jane on a couple of
occasions, but Bob had never noticed the
big cat in the window.

Bob stroked the back of her neck for a
few minutes, thinking what an incredible
experience. As he pet the cougar he began
to realize that this was not a normal
cougar. For whatever reason, it must have
been around people before. This would not
be happening if it was a wild cougar. It
seemed to him that the cougar was a
pretty hefty one too. He didn't know how
big a cougar was supposed to be, but this
one seemed pretty thick in the middle.

After some time passed it began to
grow dark. Bob knew he should get home.
He got up, put the camera bag in the pack
and slung it over his shoulder. He looked
at the cat as he walked away. The cat got
up and followed him until he reached the

trail up to the back of his house. He reached down and ran his hand across the cougars' back for a moment.

"This is where we part company. I'm sure my dad would not understand if I took you home." He started up the trail and the cat followed. Bob stopped and turned around. He held out his hand in a gesture to stop and placed the palm of his hand out, against the cougar's nose. The cat seemed to understand. It stayed there as Bob walked up the trail to his backyard. At the top of the hill Bob looked back. The cat still sat there watching him.

He entered through the back door and Buck, Marie, and Wendy were just sitting down to the dinner table.

"We were beginning to wonder if you were going to make it home in time for dinner," Marie said.

"Guess I lost track of time. I was down in the canyon gathering information for my school project." He placed a piece of baked chicken, a baked potato, with all the toppings, and some salad on his plate. He sat there, pensive for a few moments, wondering if he should say anything about the cougar. Buck had been attacked by a cougar when he saved Sally May, the girl next door, a few years ago and still had scars on his arms to prove it. Buck and Eric had also gone cougar hunting two years ago. The hunting story they'd told at the dinner table after the trip, especially the part about Soaring Eagle being attacked and nearly killed made the answer clear to him for now. He could always tell them about his experience later, but once it was out you couldn't take it back.

After dinner Bob took out the camera and hooked it up to the computer in the family room. He downloaded all the pictures and began studying them. They were mostly of the gelatinous ball and they had come out pretty good. He zoomed in on the ball and expanded it until he could see the black specks clearly. They were the eyes of whatever was inside. "Cool," he said aloud.

Buck was sitting in his recliner chair near the computer desk re-reading COUGAR ATTACKS, Encounters of the Worst Kind, by Kathy Etling. He tried to cover a multitude of topics with his Outdoor Skills class at the university and this was one subject he had spent many hours studying. In fact, he had become something of an expert on the changing behavior of cougars in the last few years. After he'd studied all of the documented cougar attacks on humans that had occurred since they began in the mid 1970's he realized that the common theory, that people were causing the attacks by moving into cougar country, simply didn't wash.

The more he studied the incidents, the less likely people seemed to be the cause. At one point he felt that he could present a pretty convincing theory that people could not possibly be the cause, with a few exceptions in southern California and the Denver, Colorado area, where the population expansions were totally out of control. The cause of the incidents, while difficult to prove, was simply an increasing cougar population. The cats were forced to move in closer to people because there was no place else for a newly dispersed young cougar to go to claim a territory of its own. That compounded with the fact that to a cougar, anything that moves is a potential food source. The incidents were bound to continue to increase.

Buck looked over at the computer monitor. "Your pictures came out pretty good." He got up and stood next to Bob looking at the monitor.

"Yeah, I found this a couple of days ago in a pool of the stream at the bottom of the canyon. It's been getting bigger each day." Bob pointed to the monitor, and zoomed in to the ball, using the cursor to point at the tiny black specks. "See these little black specks. Yesterday they were still, but today I could tell they were moving around. When I zoom in on them they look like they might be eyes."

"Could be, it isn't real clear, but if you keep going back I think you'll see what it is in a few days."

"What do you think it is?"

"Oh, I'm pretty sure I know what it is, I've seen these masses before as a kid."

"What is it?" Bob asked.

"Oh I don't want to spoil it for you. I still remember seeing it for the first time and it's pretty cool to watch it no matter how many times you've seen it."

"But maybe I'll miss it."

"Probably not if you keep going down there each day to check it out. Once it starts it goes on for awhile."

Bob realized that he hadn't taken a picture of the cougar, but he was glad he hadn't now. His dad surely would have seen it, and he'd want it out of the backyard for sure. It seemed to him like the cougar had probably been there for a while and no one had said anything about it yet, so a few more days wouldn't hurt anything. Maybe it would go away. Maybe it had just been a dream. But, he didn't think so.

Misty woke up near midnight, stretching her legs and yawned. She licked her paws then got up and climbed down the tree. She went over to the stream and lapped in the water with her raspy tongue, then headed up the side of the canyon. Once at the top she walked along the edge until she reached the six foot high cedar fence. She stood there listening for a few moments. Hearing nothing she leapt to the top of the fence then dropped down to the neatly cropped grass on the other side. The young lab that lived in the yard cowered at the edge of the house where it met the fence, trying to look small and invisible.

Misty walked casually to the back door and ate the bowl of dog food. When she had finished it she walked back toward the fence, looking over at the dog. It hadn't moved since her arrival. As long as the dogs in the backyards were doscile she ignored them, but kept an eye on them, just in case it dedided to become aggressive. If that happened it may become a meal. She crouched down and leapt up over the fence clearing it in a smooth move and landed on the trail, then walked along the edge of the canyon a few more houses and repeated the process. This was her routine every night. She recognized the dogs and cats in the backyards as possible food, but she had eaten dry cat food for years and she was accustomed to it as her primary nourishment. There was always more than enough to sustain her and it seemed unlikely that she would get hurt in the process.

The next day Bob followed the same plan after school. When he got to the bottom of the canyon he was eager to reach the pool and he began running toward it. He wanted to see what changes had occurred overnight to his mystery ball.

Misty had learned his pattern and was waiting in the brush when Bob passed her position alongside the trail. She followed him down the path. When he began running she tensed, watching him intently. When he was about fifty yards down the trail, she looked around to ensure there was no other people around, then she took off at a full run.

Bob slowed as he came to a spot where a blackberry bush had grown into the trail. He'd learned to be cautious going through the area. The thorns were sharp and caused painful infections if not removed soon enough. He thought once again, as he had yesterday, that he needed to bring some hand clippers and cut the bush away from the trail. Since he couldn't carry a knife to school there was no way to hack the daily advancing vines out of the way.

Misty halted ten feet behind Bob when he stopped. She observed then crept slowly toward him, one paw gently in front of the other as she crept through the narrowed gap.

Bob sensed something and turned around. "Hi there," he extended his hand and Misty advanced toward him and let him run his hand down her back. She pressed her side against Bob's leg.

"Let's go," Bob said, heading toward the pool and Misty followed him.

Bob laid his pack on the ground at the edge of the pool and got out the camera bag. As he extracted the camera he looked into the pool. It was a warm day and the ball was in the full sunlight. A few tadpoles swam near the mass and as he looked closer he saw one pop off the mass and swim away. He quickly took the camera and set it to the short movie setting and caught a new tadpole as it popped away from the mass. The cougar pressed against his leg, looking for attention. Bob placed his left hand on the cougar's head and stroked it, then with the camera in his right hand took more pictures. His dad was right, this was truly awesome. His dad had said he still remembered the first time he saw the tadpoles hatch. Bob would certainly remember this occasion.

Tadpoles hatching on one side and a cougar rubbing against his leg, purring, on the other. This could be the experience of a lifetime. 'Yep, this was truly an awesome experience.'

He stayed at the pool for over an hour, taking pictures and making notes. As he stroked the cougar he thought it looked especially large in the middle. Just before dark he walked back to the trail leading up to his house. Once again he held out his palm to the cougar, then headed up trail. She sat and watched as he disappeared at the top.

Misty had been searching for the right place for days. She found it just in time. That night she crawled underneath a huge rhododendron bush and back to the back. Hidden under the bush was a cave that went back into the side of the cliff about fifteen feet. It was four feet high and about ten feet wide. She circled around and around until she found the most comfortable position and then she stretched out on the ground.

At two in the morning she woke up to severe pain. She lay there panting and sweating for hours until the first kitten was born. She gently picked him up with her jaws and began licking him until he was clean, then came the second, a female. She repeated the process until the newborn female kitten was cleaned up, and then she ate the placentas. The kitten's eyes were closed, so she nudged them to her stomach where they pressed their noses around until they each found

a teat, then they greedily began to
nurse.

Bob got his driving privileges back and
was now on his old routine. He usually
drove straight home from school, had a
snack, then headed out the back door to
the watershed. For many weeks he did not
see the cougar. He was disappointed, but
was focused on his project and the
changes that were taking place. The
leaves had turned color and the branches
were now bare.

In mid November the high school
swimming team got started and it was
getting dark earlier. His trips to the
watershed were limited to the daylight
hours of the weekends.

The day after Thanksgiving it snowed
six inches. Bob decided to see what the
watershed might have to offer after a
snow. He loaded the camera and a water
bottle into his backpack, stopped at the
back door to put on duck boots, a ski
parka, snowboarding cap and gloves.

"Where you headed Bob?" Buck asked.

"I'm going to the watershed to see if
there is anything interesting for my
project after a fresh snow," he replied.

"Sounds like a good idea, have fun."

Bob smiled as he made a trail through
the snow on the back lawn. He picked up a
walking stick propped up against a tree
that Buck left by the trail, just in case
it got slippery. The trail was a gradual
incline leading to the stream at the
bottom. He looked around the watershed as
he descended. The trees were heavily

laden with snow, especially the evergreens, their bows drooping. Bob brushed against one encroaching into the trail and it started a cascading avalanche of snow from the whole tree. Bob shook himself off, thinking, 'that was kind of cool.'

Further down the trail he took the walking stick, reached it up as far as he could and gave a snowbound branch a stiff whack. The tree shed a good deal of snow in one big sigh. He repeated the game a few more times until he reached the base of the canyon. He planted the walking stick firmly in the ground at the base of the trail. The only place he figured he'd need the stick was going up and down the hill.

He was obviously the only one who had been there since the snowfall. When he arrived at the pond where he had discovered the frog eggs it had a fuzzy surface coating of snow. It was not frozen, but was getting close.

He sat back on his heels and studied everything about the pond. He did not expect to see any life in it this time of year, but he felt this unique presence at this particular place.

Then he heard the purring. He turned around and there she was, laying right behind him in the snow. He hadn't seen her for nearly two months. She was much thinner now. He worried that she was starving. He gently placed his hand on her head and ran his hand down her back. That was when he noticed that her teats were swollen with milk.

"Oh my god, you've had kittens," he said out loud. He continued to stroke her back as he looked around trying to locate them, but they were no place to be seen. He stayed there with her for over an hour until it began to snow again. It wouldn't be long until dark.

"I have to go now," he said as he got up. "I'll bring you some food tomorrow."

Saturday after breakfast Bob took an old butter container full of Scout's dog food and headed to the watershed. There was still snow on the ground, but much of it had melted away. When he got to the pond he sat back on his heels, looking in the opposite direction, hoping to see where the cougar came to him from. After waiting for fifteen minutes he decided she was not coming. He turned around to look at the pond and she was standing behind him.

"You are sneaky," he said. "Would you like something to eat?"

He opened the container and set it on the ground. She immediately ate it all. She had two kittens to feed and it was hard to find enough to eat. Making milk to feed two kittens required sustenance.

"Looks like I should have brought more. I'll bring a bigger container tomorrow."

He sat down in the snow and ran his hand across her back. She lay down next to him, laid her head down in his lap and began to purr, just like she had done with Jane.

5

Woodsey was a small town of about twelve hundred residents. There were still a few loggers working the hills, but the town residents were mostly retired loggers, a few store owners, their employees and school teachers. The town had an elementary school, but the middle school children and the high school students went to the nearest schools in Dual. The town was in the foothills at the base of the Cascade Mountain range. It was mostly an area of smaller tree farms, a hundred acres or so each. Woodsey was about five miles up river from Dual. In the seventies it had been a healthy logging town, but it had continued to lose residents each year since then because the federal rules had changed and virtually stopped all logging on federal land. The result was an immediate decline in the logging industry and the loss of thousands of jobs.

It was one o'clock in the afternoon and the mean male cougar was concealed between a huge wild blackberry bush and a low hanging cedar tree that had been trimmed numerous times over the years. It had very thick branches, but had been topped many times, so it was not tall, but more of a thick bush. The tree was at the edge of the parking lot for the Country Store Grocery Outlet.

The mean male sat between the cedar tree and the huge old blackberry bush watching as people, old and young, get in and out of the cars to do their shopping. He studied their every move, intently watching the children. Some held the hand of the bigger person that accompanied them. Others ran free around the parking lot on the way inside the building. He particularly focused on the smaller ones that separated from the bigger people. Their movements were different, more vulnerable to his modus operandi.

He caught lower movement out of the corner of his left eye. Looking in that direction he saw four dogs moving together and a lone coyote following along close behind. The pack of dogs moved together through the grocery store parking lot, crossed the street and disappeared behind a store. The cougar refocused on the comings and goings among the cars.

He had been in this area for five days straight now. There were raccoons, possums, cats, dogs and humans in abundance in this area. It was a virtual grocery store for him. He found the cats and dogs to be the easiest prey and had a cat or dog for a meal each day. He had spent about an hour each day in this parking lot watching. Sometimes the people would back their cars into the parking space next to his favorite observation point. When this happened he became very focused. When the owner returned with the groceries they always put the bags in the back of the car. The back of the vehicle was only two to three feet from where he watched the people. When there were children too he was as tense as a clock spring, as they stood only inches away from him. He could smell the shampoo fragrance in their hair.

Shortly before two in the afternoon he crouched down low and followed a game trail that led behind a block of stores. There were no big chain stores in this town. It was mostly the necessities; groceries, a gas station and mini-market at the corner up the street. A small hardware store, Rosie's gift shop and The Fly Fisherman's Paradise on this side of the street. On the street behind the stores was a row of older, small houses with good sized yards, both front and back.

As he moved slowly along behind the stores he was concealed by weeds and high grass that the store keepers didn't have time the mow. Up ahead he spotted movement, ever so slight. He crept slowly, focused on the area until he was about ten feet away. There in the high grass was a cat, creeping up on a rat that was feeding on garbage that had missed the dumpster. He tensed and sprung. The cat was so focused on the rat that it barely registered the assault. The cougar clamped his jaws down on the cat, just behind the head and the back of the neck and quickly twisted his head,

breaking the cat's spine. It wasn't dead
yet, just paralyzed, but death would come
soon.

The cougar left the cover of the grass
and walked up the street with the cat
dangling from his jaws. Just then the
pack of dogs spied him and headed toward
him at a jog, the coyote trotting along
behind. Normally a dog could make a good
meal for him, but a pack of dogs was a
different story. They took on a whole new
personality than an individual dog. A dog
alone would back away from a cat as large
as a cougar. But even normally, non
aggressive pet dogs changed when they got
the pack mentality. This pack could turn
vicious in an instant.

The dog pack was gaining on him so he
jumped a low fence into the front yard of
a house. It didn't take long for the pack
to find the gate and were inside the yard
in seconds. The mean male jumped up on
the roof of the house, the cat still
dangling from his jaws. He quickly ran up
the roof to the top and down the back
side. He jumped off the roof and landed
on the lawn, but the dogs came around the
side of the house and were only feet from
him when he took two quick steps and
jumped over the six foot fence that
surrounded the backyard. Quickly, he ran
into the woods, taking the game trail. He
ran about two hundred yards until he
began to tire. He could now hear the dogs
in pursuit. He continued until he found a
familiar maple tree and jumped up about
ten feet into the tree, then climbed up
to a large branch in the crotch of

another large branch at the trunk of the tree. The two big limbs growing side by side in the huge old maple tree created a semi-flat area about twenty square feet. He was invisible from the ground. He watched as the dogs ran up the trail, sniffing his sent. They passed under his tree at a run, then stopped about fifty yards up the trail. They turned around and passed under his tree again, then turned around once more. Near the base of his tree they wandered around for fifteen minutes, back and forth, as the cougar watched amusedly from his secure perch. Eventually the dogs lost interest and headed back to town.

The mean male began to lick the dead cat with his long raspy tongue, pulling away the skin until he could get to the sustenance inside.

The next day the cougar went to the grocery store parking lot at the same time as he had during the previous days that he had been in the area. After watching the people for about an hour he followed the trail again along behind the stores. A small dog ran across the street from a house and passed right in front of him, then went around to the front of the store. The cougar quickly followed it in pursuit. He came around the corner and saw the small dog, which immediately saw the cougar. The door to Rosie's Gift Shop opened and the small dog darted inside. As a patron left the door closed. The mean male ignored the person leaving the store as she walked, unknowingly, away from him. The cougar walked over to the window and looked inside. The dog was sitting with his backside against the counter, watching the cougar through the window. A little girl saw the cougar and went over to the window, inches away from the cat.

She said, "Mommy, look at the big kitty."

The mother came over. The cougar and the little girl were inches away from each other. The cougar stuck out his long tongue and licked his muzzle. The woman shrieked, grabbing her little girl and backed away from the window.

Rosy looked over at the window, "Oh my god!" she screamed, and grabbed her portable phone off the counter, quickly dialing 911. When asked the nature of the emergency by the 911 operator she said, "There's a cougar outside of my shop window, staring inside. We need someone here, fast." The operator took the information.

The cougar lost interest and walked to the end of the building and disappeared into the woods.

An hour and a half later Officer Wesson, of the fish and game department, arrived at Rosy's shop. He apologized for taking so long to get there but he had been sixty miles away when the call came in.

Rosy explained what had happened and gave a plausible description of the animal that the fish and wildlife officer believed was actually a cougar. The woman who had been in the store with her daughter was gone, and even though Rosy had seen her before, she did not know her name or have any way for the officer to contact her for confirmation. Officer Wesson went outside and searched the area around the store without any trace that a cougar had been in the area. He then spoke to other people on the street and Bert at the Fly Fisherman's Paradise. No one else had seen the cougar.

He returned to Rosy's shop and gave her an explanation about cougars, left her a pamphlet, his card with cell phone number and told her to call him if it was seen again.

Ruth left home at five in the morning for her job as assistant manager at the local grocery store. Two blocks from her house she stopped. A cougar lay in the middle of the road illuminated by her headlights, all stretched out. On her right was the school bus stop, right at the elementary school. She pulled up to within ten feet of the cougar, but the big cat just stretched out and looked, lazily, up at her.

"I can't believe this," she said out loud. "I've got grandchildren playing in my yard. This is ridiculous." News usually travels fast in a small town, but she had not yet heard about the cougar in town the day before, even though Rosy only lived two blocks from her.

She backed her vintage pickup truck and turned around. When she got to her home she ran into the house, to the bedroom and grabbed the .38 out of the dresser, found the shells and filled the cylinder. She had hunted with her husband when she was younger and was familiar with the pistol. She left the house without waking her husband, who had worked the late shift last night at the local Stop and Go Mini-mart and gas station. He's been working there for the last year since he had lost his job as a logger.

She jumped in the truck and headed back to the school bus stop. She was focused, she had a mission. But, when she got there, the cougar was gone. She got out of the truck and looked around. The sun was not up yet, but the morning twilight was now providing enough light to see. Getting back in the truck she looked around the area. When she was unable to locate the big cat she proceeded on to work, the pistol laying on the seat next to her.

In the meantime, the cougar had wandered through the neighborhood. Walking around the perimeter of some of the houses, then he walked through the woods back to his favorite maple tree. He crouched down and jumped all the way up to the crotch in the huge branches and stretched out for a nap.

A country grocery store is a place where a lot of local people go every day. That day Ruth told everyone she saw, and she knew most everyone that shopped in the store, about the cougar at the bus stop. Not one had heard about the cougar at Rosy's. Ruth did not report the incident to any of the authorities.

That afternoon the cougar repeated his afternoon routine. He slinked into the cover of the cedar tree at the edge of the grocery store parking lot shortly after noon and watched the patrons for over an hour. It was a rainy day and all the patrons hurried from the cars to the store and returned just as quickly, stowing the groceries hurriedly in the back seat and departed. There were not as many people that day, especially the children. He lost interest and headed back through the grass, crouching down and moving slowly. The rain did not affect his routine.

He sensed movement again today at the same place off to his right. The poodle ran across the street passing twenty feet in front of him and disappeared around the side of the store. This time he was ready. He was in hot pursuit immediately. When he turned the corner at the side of the store the poodle was standing at the door. The dog immediately saw the cougar and began frantically scratching at the door. The cougar was swift this time, taking two quick steps he had the dog in his jaws. His canine teeth penetrated between the vertebra, then he shifted his grip chomping down and shifting the jaw and teeth position. The dog went limp.

As he began walking to the corner of the building the door to the shop opened.

Rosy saw her dog dangling from the cougars jaws. "Oh no, stop!" she ran out of the store toward the cat ready to give it a stiff kick, when the cougar turned

around. It's eyes menacing, he gave a
hiss. Rosy backed off, and the cat
disappeared around the corner. She went
to the corner and watched the big cat
walk across the street, past the houses
and into the woods.

She ran to the Fly Fisherman's
Paradise. "Burt, a cougar just got my
dog, right in front of the store. I
watched it carry Muffy off into the
woods."

Burt opened a drawer under the counter
and pulled out a Smith & Wesson .9mm and
went out the door heading toward the
woods.

Rosy retuned to her store and called
Officer Wesson using the number he left
with his card. She got a recording and
left a message. Twenty minutes later he
returned her call, apologizing for the
delayed return of her call, but he had
been out of cell phone coverage.

Burt returned to his store and placed
his .9mm back in the top drawer. He then
walked over to Rosy's, "Sorry Rosy, but I
didn't see anything. Went about a mile
back into the woods on the game trail. I
didn't even see a drop of blood."

"Thanks Burt," she said sadly, just as
Officer Wesson pulled up in front of
Rosy's.

Officer Wesson walked into the store.
"So it was back again today?"

"The damned thing killed my dog. I
watched it walk away with Muffy in his
jaws. It even turned around and hissed at
me when I tried to stop it."

Officer Wesson asked her questions and repeated a search of the same area as yesterday, with no sign of any kind that a cougar had been there. Once again there were no other witnesses. When he returned to Rosy's store about two hours later he said, "Please call me immediately if you, or anyone else, sees it. I'm sorry about the loss of your dog ma'am."

The next day the cougar repeated the same routine. At ten minutes after two in the afternoon Rosy looked out the front window of the store, and there was the cougar, nose pressed up against the window looking in at her. She was the only person in the store at the time. The cougar placed his huge paw up on the window, pressing to see if he could get in. Rosy picked up the portable phone off the counter and dialed 911, then walked over closer to the window while waiting for the operator to come on the line.

The cougar looked intently at Rosy and then slid out his long tongue and licked his chops, twice.

Rosy jumped back just as the operator said. "911 what is the nature of your emergency?"

"This is Rosy at Rosy's Gift Shop in Woodsey. The cougar is back again."

"One moment, I'll connect you with the fish and game department."

"No! I want the sheriff this time. The fish and game guy takes over an hour to get here and it's always gone by time he gets here. I want the sheriff, he'll be here within minutes."

"Hold one minute, please stay on the line," was the response.

She explained the situation to the sheriff's office dispatcher and he said there was an officer on the way. She then called Officer Wesson's cell phone and got a recorded message. When the beep came she said, "Hi Officer Wesson, it's Rosy. It's two thirty and the cougar is back again. Sheriff's on the way too this time," and hung up.

Ten minutes later the sheriff pulled up in front of Rosy's and she went outside as he was getting out of the car. "The cougar went around the corner of the building about ten minutes ago. I watched it walk that way," pointing to the houses behind main street.

"Okay, I'll have a look around," he said.

He got back into his SUV and began driving through the housing area. Ten minutes later he saw the cougar walking down the middle of the street, houses on both sides.

He got on the radio and called in that he was in Woodsey and he had the cougar in sight. The sergeant came on the radio and said, "Shoot it if you can get a clear shot that doesn't endanger anyone or property."

"Okay," the deputy responded.

The deputy was young. He had been on the force for a little over a year. He was not necessarily an animal lover and he understood the danger of a cougar in the middle of town, but it was a small town, in cougar country. He drove up right behind the big cat. The cougar turned around at the sound of the approaching SUV, looked it over and then continued on walking up the middle of the street.

The deputy honked the horn. The cougar looked back again, this time there was a different look in his eyes, like defiance. The cougar walked into the front yard of one of the houses. The deputy realized his mistake of being impatient, too late. He got out of the car and drew his service semi-automatic .9mm pistol. When he advanced on the cougar the front door of the house opened and a middle aged woman stepped out onto the porch.

"What's going on?" she yelled.

"Get back in the house lady, there's a cougar in your front yard," the deputy responded.

She looked to her left and saw the cat. It was about thirty feet away. She was mesmerized. She was a high school teacher at home on a sick day. She'd never seen a cougar before outside of the zoo.

The deputy was not in a position to safely get a shot off.

At the sight of the woman on the porch the cougar decided this was too many humans focused on him, and too close. He crouched down and instantly sprang up onto the roof of the house. He disappeared over the top of the roof to the other side in the blink of an eye.

The deputy ran around the house. At the same time the school teacher ran

through the house and opened the back
door. The cougar had jumped off the roof
and was standing in the middle of the
backyard when the deputy came around the
corner. He raised his gun.

"No, don't shoot it," the woman
yelled.

The deputy looked over at the woman,
then quickly back to the cougar, but it
was gone.

"I don't want you to hurt it," she
exclaimed.

He ran around behind the fence and
into the woods, but it had disappeared,
like a breath in the wind. He wasn't too
keen on trying to track it down by
himself.

When he got back to his SUV the woman
came out of the house again.

"You weren't going to shoot it were
you?" she asked.

"It's dangerous for a cougar to be in
town. There are people and kids around
here and it's been hanging around for
three days now, that we know of. Who
knows, maybe it's been here for weeks."

"That's still no reason to hurt it.
Take it back into the woods where it
belongs."

"Only the fish and game people can do
that, and they haven't had much luck with
that method anyway, they just come back."

The deputy drove back to Rosy's and found
the fish and game SUV just pulling up.
They both got out and the sheriff's
deputy explained to Officer Wesson what
had taken place.

Wesson told the deputy he would take it from there. He'd call out the dog handlers and go after it. The deputy said thanks for the help and left.

Officer Wesson called two different cougar dog trackers in an attempt to get some help to track down the cougar. Each was a dead end. He then called his immediate supervisor, Sergeant Smith, on his cell phone.

"Sergeant Smith," Came the answer.

"Hi it's Wesson, I'm back in Woodsey. It was here again this afternoon. The sheriff deputy beat me here. He followed it through town, then tried to track it into the woods, but didn't have any luck."

"You better get some hounds out there," Sergeant Smith responded.

"That's why I'm calling. I just talked with them both and they say they are at work and don't have time for it," Wesson explained.

"Did you offer them the fifty dollar fee?"

"Yeah, they both got a good laugh out of that. They each said it isn't worth the trouble for less than five hundred dollars, per day."

"Five hundred dollars, that's ridiculous," Sergeant responded.

"Yeah, and there's still no guarantee they'll get it."

"Okay, you need to be there tomorrow, all day," Sergeant Smith directed. "It's been there at around two in the afternoon each day. Scout the town out and look for places you think it might be hanging out and maybe where it is spending the night. I'll try to be there in the early afternoon too."

Officer Wesson went into Rosy's. "Hi."

"Hi," she responded.

"Have you heard of any more animals missing or anything else about the cougar happening around town in the last few days?" he asked.

"No nothing, just that it was back at my window at ten after two this afternoon. It's kind of unnerving, that thing hanging around town like this. Keeps the customers away," she said.

"I'll be here all day tomorrow," he declared. "Please give me a call immediately if anyone sees it."

"Okay," she answered.

The next day Officer Wesson arrived at six in the morning and began cruising around the town looking for signs of the cougar. At eight he parked the SUV and walked up the game trail that bordered the houses. He walked for about two miles, but found no cougar signs. Back at the SUV, he resumed cruising around the town.

Shortly after noon he positioned the light green fish and game SUV a block away from Rosy's where he had a panoramic view of the whole area on Main Street.

At one o'clock officer Wesson noticed movement in his rear view mirror as Sergeant Smith pulled up behind him. Wesson got out and went back to talk with him. Smith rolled down his window.

"See anything yet?" Sergeant Smith asked.

"Nothing at all. I've been sitting here for about an hour. Checked all over town earlier this morning. Even went out into the woods on a game trail that seemed like a logical trail for it to be using. Went in over a mile and didn't find any signs of cougar activity."

"Where do you think it's coming in?" Smith inquired.

"Rosy, the lady that owns that shop over there," he said, pointing at Rosy's Gift Shop, "said it departs around that corner of the building each time," he pointed at the west side of the building. There's a trail in the grass behind the building indicating it comes in on the east side of the building and probably leaves on the west side. There is also a game type trail in the grass that leads to the bushes at the back side of the grocery store."

"Okay, you stay here and I'll drive around back there to see if it turns up."

At five in the afternoon Sergeant Smith pulled up next to Wesson and pressed the button to run down the passenger window. "Looks like a no show," Smith said.

"Sure does, I'll stick around for another hour. If it doesn't show by then I'll call it a day."

"Good plan," said Smith. "See you tomorrow," and he drove away.

At six Officer Wesson yawned, stepped out of the SUV and walked over to Rosy's. He opened the door and stepped in.

"Hi," he said. "I'd guess the cougar may have moved on. I searched the trail behind the housing area this morning without any cougar sign. You said it was here every day at about two, and it didn't show today. Cougars are animals that have defined habit patterns. They typically stay in an area for three to six days and then move on. I haven't seen any deer or signs of deer here today, and deer are the primary food source for cougars. It seems likely to me that it moved on."

"What if it hasn't?" Rosy asked.

"Call me and I'll be back as soon as I can."

"That's reassuring, I'll call the sheriff first. He got here in ten minutes after I called 911, it took you over an hour to get here."

"Fish and game resources are limited and we cover very large geographical areas. We do the best we can."

"Well to be honest with you, I don't care who kills it. I just want to see it dead. It ain't right for a cougar to be walking around town eatin' people's pets. We ignore this and it'll be eatin' our kids next."

"Whenever we have to kill a cougar the animal rights people descend on Olympia and create a lot of political problems."

"What are those idiots thinking? Animals are just part of the food chain," Rosy stated.

"Guess you found that out yesterday," Wesson said.

"Touché, I'll miss Muffy, but not as much as if one of the kids around here was taken. Those buffoons in the city are making rules for those of us who live out in the country. That can never work."

The night before the cougar had tired of existing on a paltry diet of cats and dogs. It was minimal sustenance for him. It worked for a few days, but he needed a lot more to eat. At ten in the evening he had reluctantly left his comfortable perch high in the crotch of the huge maple tree. He had been able to stretch out and relax completely in this expanse between the huge boughs of the old tree. He could lay out flat, even stretch out and be completely concealed from anyone passing on the ground.

He jumped the twenty feet to the ground, walked through the woods, through the housing area, across the main street of town, down into the river bed and began hunting up river.

Moving along a game trail in the early twilight of the next evening he stopped and looked out into the riverbed. A deer was bent down on its front legs getting a drink out of the river. The cougar crouched down and began creeping slowly toward the deer. Twenty feet away the deer stood up and looked back over it's shoulder. The deer bolted, the rocks and gravel flew as the cougar took three steps and leaped, sailing through the air he landed on the back of the deer. He quickly fastened his jaws behind the back of the head, clamping his teeth down on the neck and twisting his head. The deer dropped like a stone.

He easily dragged the one hundred fifty pound deer out of the riverbed and into the brush at the edge of the watershed. He continued until he found a place that was concealed from the game trail under the dense low hanging boughs of a Douglas fir tree. Inside he began licking the underbelly with his raspy tongue. The hair pulled quickly away from the skin, and exposed the soft hide. After chewing a hole through the skin the cougar ripped open the stomach cavity and carefully removed the intestines, placing them in a neat pile, three feet from the carcass. He ate the heart first, then the liver and lungs for the high nutrient value. Hours later he began feeding on the rest of the deer. He had been eating only sparsely for the last week. He consumed over thirty pounds of the deer in the first few hours.

6

Gretchen Wortz lived in a filthy, run down old trailer with flat tires, parked in a seedy trailer park. The park was all asphalt, without a single tree and very few plants, other than the weeds that grew up through the asphalt. Rusted old pickup trucks and beat up, dirty cars lined the streets next to the assortment of trailers and dilapidated mobile homes. Occasionally, insulation could be seen exuding from the side of an old fashon, metal mobile home where the siding had fallen off from maintenance neglect. Some of the vehicles in the park still ran, others just sat there gathering dust, waiting to be towed to the junkyard.

Gretchen's mother was an alcoholic and brought home a different man nearly every night from the tavern she frequented. Gretchen only went to school occasionally. There was no one at the school who seemed to care if she was there or not. She was a little on the slow side because her mother, who was only sixteen when she was born, had been on drugs while she was pregnant with her. The other kids at school made fun of her because she was usually dirty and smelly. Most days she chose not to go to school and her mother was rarely up early enough

to make her go to school. By the time her
mother got up, they both figured why
bother, it was too late to go to school
anyway. Her grades were poor, but she
didn't care and her mother could care
less.

Shortly after Gretchen turned twelve
her mother brought home new clothes and
made her take a bath every day. Her
mother began selling her to the men she
brought home. It was an easy way to pay
for booze and the trailer space rent. One
night when she was fourteen years old her
mother brought home a man who beat them
both into unconsciousness before leaving.

Three days later, having recovered
from the beating she watched her mother
leave for the bar at four in the
afternoon. Gretchen packed as many of her
clothes as she could into her school
backpack, grabbed her jacket off the hook
and walked out the front door of the
trailer for the last time. A block away
she turned and looked back at the rusted
hulk and the flat tires, then turned and
walked into the darkness of the night.

She walked about a mile to the freeway
and found an overpass. There were a lot
of bushes and places to hide under the
overpass and it would be dry if it
started to rain. She found a large
rhododendron with a canopy and a space
large enough underneath it for her to lie
down and sleep. She crawled in, scared
and feeling helpless, curled up her legs
under her and pulled the jacket hood up
over her head. It took her awhile to get

comfortable and she was exhausted. She
finally fell asleep.

It was a long night with little sleep.
She was cold when the sun started coming
up and she realized there were other
people there too, most seemed to be teens
also. They were starting a fire in an old
fifty-five gallon drum. She went over and
stood next to the fire and met some of
the others.

She quickly learned that most of the
teens there had experienced a variety of
problems at home before striking out on
their own. They would sleep underneath a
freeway bridge at night. It was dry, and
usually warmer than sleeping in the woods
when the night was especially cold or
rainy. That afternoon she and her new
found friends drank, smoked some grass, a
few were doing meth. Once on the street
with the other homeless kids and older
men and women it wasn't long before she
acquired a drug habit. She made a few
bucks hooking and begging. It was usually
enough to buy whatever drugs were
available, usually meth, but she'd tried
heroin a couple of times. Most days she
sucked at a twenty-four ounce can of malt
liquor until dusk. If she had managed to
make enough to buy a hit of whatever was
available she'd shoot up when it got
dark.

Gretchen was now twenty-two years old.
She could have easily passed for forty.
Her eyes were deep set with an empty, far
away gaze. They were bordered by heavy
crow's feet trailing away from the
corners. She was missing two front teeth

and didn't even care. Two years ago she'd been diagnosed HIV positive at the Free Clinic. It wasn't an unusual plight for a homeless woman, considering her multiple partners over the years. It could have come from one of the shared needles. It might have been one of the numerous times she'd been beaten and raped by one or more of the homeless druggies. It could have been when she was hooking a few years ago. Hooking was history now. She rarely found willing customers anymore because of her poor hygiene and unhealthy appearance. It was a reality of life for homeless women, but most of them, like Gretchen had given up caring. It was just a tool of survival for women. The fact that she was passing on the HIV disease was immaterial to her. Her life couldn't get much worse. Between the booze and the drugs her brain barely functioned much of the time.

One day last week she woke up near noon with a whopping hangover. Sitting up holding her head she looked around. The cars overhead on the bridge sounded thunderous and she could see a river in front of her. Close by she saw a sleeping bag under a blue tarp and two small makeshift cardboard enclosures. Probably used as a place to sleep, either for privacy or to help keep the cold away. There were two more, larger sets of blue tarps above and below people sleeping in an area away from the bridge that was surrounded by a dozen or more smaller trees. The tarps had been tied to the trees to form a makeshift tent. There was also a tattered tent a little farther away past the trees, nearly invisible, hidden in high grass and bushes.

She vaguely remembered getting into a car last night and she thought, there'd been a promise of money. She couldn't even remember who was in the car, but she vaguely remembered two or three men in it with her. She smelled smoke and looked around seeing a group of homeless people sitting on the ground next to a small campfire. She went over to the fire and sat down next to a woman. Gretchen held her throbbing head in her hands. She looked over at the woman sitting next to her, who looked to be about her age.

"Where are we?" Gretchen asked.

"Dual. It's a small town about fifty miles northeast of Seattle." She stuck her hand out, "They call me Buzzy, cause I always got a buzz on." Gretchen noticed a twenty-four ounce can of beer between her knees.

"Hi, I'm Gretchen."

"That your real name?" Buzzy asked.

"Yeah."

"Your mom must not have liked you very much. Bet the kids at school made fun of you. I guess thirty years ago that was a pretty common name. But, I never met anyone named Gretchen before."

"Yeah, my mom had problems. She was only sixteen when I was born."

"Most people around here go by some kind of nickname. I'll see if I can think one up for you. How'd you end up here?"

"I don't really know. I vaguely remember getting into a car last night, and here I am."

Buzzy began laughing hysterically.

"What's so funny?" Gretchen asked.

"That's exactly how I got here," the young woman answered. "I got drunk as a skunk one night. Some guys promised me a good time and some money. Next day I woke up under this bridge. But you know what? It's a lot better here than it was when I was in Seattle. You can get good handouts just standing on the corner. Plenty of money to buy beer and booze. There's a fast food place across the street. You can get all the food you want for free."

"How do you do that? I'm starving." Gretchen declared.

"Come on I'll show you. I could use something to eat myself."

Gretchen hadn't eaten anything for days. She and Buzzy went to the back of a fast food restaurant across the street and went dumpster diving. They lifted the lid to the dumpster and took out a big tied plastic bag, carrying it back to the campsite. Sitting on the ground at the base of a tree, they opened the bag and began scavenging through the trash, removing food that had been discarded. It was amazing how much food was thrown away. One bag contained more than the whole congregation of homeless people under the bridge could eat. Some of the other homeless people from the tent area joined in and they all had a family meal together.

After eating Buzzy said, "Come on, I'll show you how it works. After today you have to find your own corner though." She picked up a two foot square piece of cardboard that said,

'LOST EVERYTHING IN A FIRE.
GOT LITTLE KIDS. PLEASE HELP.
GOD BLESS.'

The others slowly picked up their cardboard signs, with 'PLEASE HELP' or some other slogan written on them and went their separate ways to find a corner where they could stand, asking passing cars for handouts. Food was plentiful for these homeless people, unlike where she had been in Seattle. The homeless people there constantly fought among themselves. Occasionally, the fights would require hospitalization. There was even a dead body found one morning in the area they all camped last year. That brought the police in and they broke up the whole encampment area. She had found a new place to sleep for two weeks and then they all had reclaimed the old camp area after the death was forgotten.

This place was different. These people seemed to help each other out occasionally with beer money when they had a bad day, or were too hung over to stand on a corner. Buzzy told her that drugs were hard to come by in this town.

By ten that night Gretchen had a buzz on from drinking high alcohol content malt liquor all day, she staggered away from the crowd that hovered around the

blazing campfire. A half dozen sleeping
bags were already in use near the
campfire. It was a cool evening and
they'd need the heat to help make it
through the night. She headed for the
cover of foliage at the edge of the
riverbank, she felt awful, knowing she
was going to be sick again. Trying to
think, she knew she'd drank four or five,
maybe it was six or seven, cans of
twenty-four ounce malt liquor since
waking up around noon. Maybe it was
something she ate, it didn't really
matter, it was happening frequently since
she'd arrived there.

The mean male cougar had followed the
watershed to the place where it emptied
into the much larger river. He slinked
along the bank of the river, his strength
clearly visible in the rippling of the
leg muscles as he walked. His head up,
eyeing the area ahead, searching from
side to side as he slowly made his way.
Blackberry bushes hung over the lip of
the riverbed and grew down to the edge of
the river in some places. They provided
both food and cover for many of the
animals that populated the watershed.
Deer were especially fond of the thorny
plant, as with many other thorny plants,
especially roses. One deer can wipe out a
carefully tended backyard rose garden
overnight.
     It was four o'clock in the afternoon
with still plenty of daylight left.
Instinctively, the cougar knew it was
time to hunt for prey. It was the time

when most animals began to forage, especially deer.

A year and a half ago Swawa, his mother, had returned from a hunting trip after leaving her six month old kittens behind. During her absence the male runt of the litter had began playfully batting at his much larger brother. The playfulness had eventually turned into a full fledged fight. When Swawa returned dragging a raccoon into the cover of the blackberry bush the female kittens sat watching in horror as their bigger brother ate their smaller brother. Swawa dropped the raccoon and lashed out at the mean male kitten, slashing a gash across his front left quarter. The mean male lashed back with a vengeance, but the three female kittens, not wanting to suffer a similar fate, took sides with the mother and joined in, forcing him out of the temporary home.

Four against one, the mean male fled the cover of the blackberry bushes. He sat outside for two hours then tried to return to share the raccoon, but was repelled by all four cougars. He hung around the area for three days, but each time he tried to rejoin his family he was re-buffed. Resigned to his fate he left the area and began wandering. Six months was a young age for a cougar to be expected to survive on his own, but he was determined, resourceful and had learned well from what little hunting skills Swawa had passed on to him.

The mean male cat then headed down the mountain and within three days found a trail alongside a stream. As the stream worked its way downhill it eventually turned into a watershed bordered by houses on each side at the top of the canyon. He traveled from the base of the Cascade Mountains down through the increasingly populated area, through the border of the Seattle suburbs until it emptied into the Puget Sound. The first time he arrived at the edge of the Sound he determined this to be his home range. From the base of the mountains to where the watershed poured into the big river was over ten miles long.

The watershed was used by a few joggers, morning or evening walkers and occasionally children out for a bike ride or a run through the stream on a hot summer day, but sections of the area could go for weeks without any use by humans. Off the main trail by the stream it was mostly dense growth with game trails leading through the foliage. The trail along the stream was used by people and game. As he traveled the route through the game trail in the brush, back and forth, the trail gradually changed over time and enlarged to accommodate his size. He used this trail to travel, concealed, and also to observe the main trail along the stream. He roamed the bottom of the watershed, sometimes by day, but usually at night.

In the first year he survived mainly by eating raccoons, rabbits, possums and occasionally a deer. After he had been living in the watershed for about thirteen months the smaller animals that lived there were all consumed by the cougar and it became increasingly difficult for him to find prey. As he searched the boundaries of his area he began ascending the sometimes steep, densely foliated sides of the watershed in search of new prey. Sometimes he would encounter a fence separating the watershed from the houses and apartments that bordered it. Other times the resident had left the backyard natural to enjoy the beauty of the trees and shrubs. He soon learned that the places where there were fences frequently had dogs in the backyard, hence the fence to keep it contained. As he walked along behind the fence he could occasionally sense the presence of a dog on the other side. Other times he would jump up into a tree to see if the backyard contained a dog for a meal.

At night he could see people inside some of the houses walking around or sitting watching TV. This usually caught his attention and sometimes he would lay in the tree and watch the people for hours, observing their behavior. He was keenly interested in watching the smaller people, the children. Their movements and mannerisms suggested they would be easier prey.

When he was a year and a half old he weighed one hundred and ten pounds, and he was a very aggressive cougar. He had quickly learned to modify his hunting habits and survived mainly on dogs, and

occasionally cats from the backyards of
the houses bordering the watershed. His
home range was now over one hundred
square miles. It went from the base of
the Cascades to the point where the ever
increasing size of the stream at the
bottom of the watershed emptied into the
river and eventually the Sound. He was
now expanding his home range to include
another watershed that also emptied into
the same big river. This watershed was
about three miles up the big river from
the watershed he originally staked out as
his home range. As he roamed up and down
the natural area he knew which yards he
had been successful at finding prey. In
time he also learned that those yards
usually had a new dog within a few months
after he had secured a meal there. For
over a year he had managed to feed
himself well by raiding backyards in the
middle of the night. Just because there
wasn't an animal present, that didn't
mean there wouldn't be a bowl of food set
out.

In time the smaller animal prey
disappeared. After a period of two weeks
when he was unable to find a single dog,
cat, raccoon or possum he focused on the
point where the big river flowed into the
Sound. He climbed the trail to the rim of
the watershed and discovered an alley
behind a tall building. A huge trash bin
was overflowing and the whole length of
the alley was cluttered with debris. A
rat, the size of a house cat, scurried
around the trash eating whatever was
edible. The cougar crouched and slowly

made its way forward until it was fifteen feet away. Tense, tail twitching he jumped the distance, but the rat sensed the attack and fled to the safety of a crack in the crumbling side of an old building.

The cougar easily leapt up on top of the dumpster, lay down and looked over the edge, patiently waiting. Only minutes later another equally large rat appeared, quickly followed by another, and then another. Raising up slightly, he dropped off the dumpster swinging his left paw at the fleeing rat, knocking it into the side of the building. Slightly dazed, the rat was slow to respond. The cat batted it again, knowing it was trapped and could not escape. The rat bared its teeth and screeched at the big cat. The cougar swiped at it again, this time slicing a gash in its left side and slinging it into the corner between the two walls. The rat bared its teeth again, screeching as it tried to attack the cat, only to be impaled by three sharp claws and pinned to the ground. The rat struggled, trying to free itself, trying to bite the big cat, but the cougar pressed the rat with it's large paw, increasing the pressure slowly against the wall, keeping the sharp teeth away from himself until the rat died. Releasing the rat the cat took it in his jaws and retreated to the watershed. He found a clump of blackberry bushes and slid into the open space underneath. Once out of sight he removed the intestines, neatly placing them to the side and ate the rat.

He stayed around the area for two weeks repeating the process each night until he was unable to find any more rats or mice. After a few days of unsuccessful hunting in the area he moved back into the big riverbed and traveled a short distance to a small watershed he had never used before.

It was a Friday evening and he heard noise at the top of the watershed. Curious, he climbed up the side until he reached a steep cliff. The lip of the cliff was about twenty feet above him, but he could see a clear area right at the edge. Crouched down he leaped up, front feet landing over the edge and he easily pulled his hind feet up and over. A well tended, landscaped area covered a space for about ten feet in from the cliff and held numerous types of plants ranging from flowering plants to smaller trees. In the darkness his keen night vision made it easy for him to see, yet be unseen as he moved in the bushes.

Nearby was a fraternity house and adjacent to it was another large, well tended yard. College men and women stood around the building drinking and smoking while others wandered around inside the fraternity house.

An intoxicated male member of the party staggered over to the edge of the cliff. It was dark and he had to relieve himself. Unzipping his pants, he held onto a small tree trunk with his left hand, as the urine flowed over the cliff.

The cougar watched closely, about twenty feet from the man. Crouched down he slowly crept closer until he was less than ten feet away. Trembling, twitching his tail, the cougar watched the man sway back and forth as the urine continued to flow. Tensing, he was ready to pounce.

"Hey Ralph," a fraternity brother yelled, walking toward him.

"Over here," Ralph called out.

The cougar saw peripheral movement, gazing past the urinating man, he saw another man approaching. Edging backward, he belly-crawled until he was camouflaged behind a rhododendron bush. He watched the new arrival following suit, watering the plants. When finished the two men walked away together. There were still people milling about when he noticed a woman smoking near the front of the building. Slowly he crept nearer until he was only ten feet behind her. He tensed his muscles, tail twitching back and forth.

Suddenly the door flew open and a group of men came out talking loudly. They all gathered at the bottom of the steps swinging beer bottles, laughing and talking loudly. Concealed by the darkness the cougar again slowly belly crawled backward until he was covered by foliage. He slinked off to the edge of the watershed and jumped down from the ledge, disappearing into the night. He slept under a large mountain laurel bush, a plant with beautiful small white star shaped flowers with maroon streaks through the petals. It was a common plant in the mountains of the east, but not the west. It had probably been planted there by someone many years ago. After a few hours of rest, hunger took over and he emerged to search for prey once again. He headed down the watershed all night until he came to a main river. After sleeping most of the day he traveled upriver all of the next night and some of the following day only finding a raccoon on the second night. On the third night he found a smaller river feeding into the larger river and followed it upstream for a full day.

Sometime after midnight the sound of a crackling fire caught his attention and he climbed the side of the hill to investigate. Hunkered down low to the ground he crawled through the bushes until he could see people around a fire in a big metal can. In his previous observations of humans, the movements of the smaller ones made them seem more vulnerable. But all of these people seemed to walk in an unusual way. This caught his attention immediately. Some staggered, others stumbled, almost any one of them looked like a possible target. But they were all too close together, and that would not do. He watched the people for hours, some gradually lay down near the fire until there was only three of them still up. He lay in the darkness keenly focused on the people when a woman headed toward him.

Gretchen felt awful. Knowing she was going to be sick again, she headed away from the fire barrel toward the edge of the woods at the top of the river bank and dropped to her knees. Almost immediately she spewed the burgers and fries from her earlier dumpster diving haul over the edge of the ravine. She remained on her knees after her stomach was finally empty, waiting for the pain and convulsing to stop.

The cougar watched the woman intensely. He was only four feet from her, tense as a clock spring, like a snake ready to strike.

Gretchen raised one leg to get up, but was knocked backwards, intense pain washed through her as the cougar's upper jaw chomped down on her head. Her scalp peeled from the occipital protuberance at the back of her head up over her head and covered her face.

The mean male pulled back and instinctively lunged again, this time taking her entire head in his jaws. His lower jaw pressed against her throat. Backing into the bushes he pulled her until they were out of sight of the people. Turning around, he dragged her down the hill into the watershed. Gretchen couldn't even scream. Her mouth was covered by the cougar's mouth and her jaws wouldn't open because its teeth were securely clamped on the back of her head, and her throat. He dragged her down the trail until he reached the bottom of the watershed. It was dark and there was no activity around. Dropping his prey he licked the side of her face with his raspy tongue, peeling away skin in the process, the wound giving up fresh, warm blood.

Three days later the mean male cougar left the lower end of the watershed immediately after caching Gretchen. He headed east into the upper end of his roaming area.

After five days of unsuccessful hunting he awoke at four in the afternoon. He stretched his legs from the branch he had been sleeping on and climbed down twenty feet to the ground. It was time to hunt for food. Moving up the side of the watershed he soon reached the lip of the canyon. He walked slowly toward a house. A few years ago the area had all been part of the forest, but today there were nice, big new homes. Most of them were on large lots, some as much as five acres. The watershed bordered many of the new houses. He walked along the area that was a buffer zone between the backyards and the watershed. Walking past a waterfall, he climbed the trail to the top and found a neatly manicured, grassy area. He continued along bordering the houses and the woods, passing a half dozen houses before he came across a potential prey.

7

John Paul left his backyard to walk his
black lab as he did every morning before
work. He decided they'd go down the trail
into the watershed today. They hadn't
gone that way for over a week. When they
reached the bottom of the canyon he
released the snap on the dog's collar.

"Okay Duke, go for it."

The dog took off at a full run heading
down the trail along the side of the
stream, stopping to sniff occasionally.
Fifteen minutes into the walk the dog
started to bark. It was normal for him to
disappear while on the outings, but he
didn't usually bark much. John couldn't
see the dog so he continued walking
toward Duke until he could saw him about
twenty feet off the main trail. He walked
over to Duke and found what had got his
attention. He could plainly see two shoes
attached to two legs. The rest of the
body was covered with leaves and
branches. He moved closer to make sure of
what he was seeing. He stood about three
feet from the body for a few minutes not
believing what he was seeing. As the
reality of his discovery hit home he
quickly felt sick to his stomach.
Dropping to his knees he gave up his

breakfast in a series of spasmodic convulsions.

John walked back to the main trail, leaving Duke sniffing around the body. John pulled out his cell phone with a shaky hand, pushed 911 and then the send button.

"Nine-one-one," came the voice of a female emergency communications operator. "What is the nature of your emergency? Do you want ambulance, fire or police?"

He thought for a moment, not anticipating the questions. His mind was clouded with thoughts of what he had just discovered.

"I think I want police."

"One moment please."

"Sheriff's department," the male dispatcher said. "What is the nature of your emergency?"

"I just found a dead body."

"Do you believe it to be a human body?"

"Yes, it's definitely human. I could see the legs in a pair of denim pants, shoes at the end of the pants."

"Are you sure that the person is dead?"

"It's mostly covered with leaves and sticks, but I can't imagine that it would be alive."

John gave the desk duty officer his name, cell phone number and his home phone number and explained his location.

"Please hold the line while I dispatch a deputy to your location."

"Okay, I'll hold."

Two minutes later the 911 operator came back on, "Is the body male or female?" the dispatcher asked. He needed to keep the caller on the line until the deputy was on the scene.

"I can't really tell, all I can see is the feet and a few inches of jeans material." He left the trail and moved back closer to the body so he could see it again. "From the size of the shoes I'd guess it's female, but that's just a guess."

After five minutes of talking on the phone he said, "I can hear a siren approaching, sounds like it is getting close."

The dispatcher relayed information to the responding first officer on the scene. Soon John could see the officer standing at the top of the canyon about one hundred yards up the canyon.

"I can see the officer standing at the top of the watershed," he said to the dispatcher. "He's about one hundred yards south of me." He waved at the officer and hollered, "I'm down here!"

"Okay, I see you," the officer responded. "Stay right there please." Soon he could hear more sirens arriving.

In the next ten minutes three more officers arrived.

"The one wearing Sergeant's stripes asked, "Are you John Paul?"

"Yes sir I am."

"I'm Sergeant Williams, King County Sheriff's Department. I understand you think you've found a human body."

"That's correct."

"Are you still on the line with the dispatcher?"

"Yes," John Paul responded.

"Could I speak with him for a moment?"

"Sure," and he handed his cell phone to the officer.

"Hi, this is Sergeant Williams. I'll take it from here." He turned off the cell phone and handed it back to John Paul. "Thank you sir. Can you show us where the body is now?"

"Yes, it's right over there," pointing toward the area where the body lay. "I'd rather not go back to it if that's okay with you."

"Sure no problem, I understand. We'd like you to stay right here while we go over to investigate. I'm going to have some questions for you in a few minutes."

"Yeah, no problem. I need to call my office. I'm not going to be at work on time.

"Alright, go ahead. We'll be right back."

The four officers went over to the area John had pointed to, finding the dog still there sniffing around the body.

The sergeant dusted the leaves away from the head to make sure it was really a dead body. "Oh god," he grimaced.

Convinced it was a dead body, he took out his cell phone and notified the dispatcher to send the county Medical Examiner to the scene.

To the other officers he said, "Seal off the area for about fifty yards in all directions. Don't get any closer to the victim until the Medical Examiner's has a chance to check out the scene.

"Sir, could you call your dog over there. I don't want it disrupting anything the Medical Examiner and our investigation team might uncover."

"Duke!" the man yelled. Duke picked up his ears then padded over to John.

Kim Chee arrived at the top of the watershed in the marked county Medical Examiner's van. The street had a police car parked sideways to keep the lookie loos and reporters away from the scene.

He stopped at the road block and to the officer he said, "Hi, I'm from the Medical Examiner's office. I'm here to pick up a body."

"You can park over there by the police vehicles," responded the officer on duty at the roadblock. "You're going to have to walk down to the crime scene though."

Kim parked and looked over the edge. He quickly assessed that this was not going to be much fun. Kim was a bit overweight. Making his way down wouldn't be bad, but getting back up with a body on a stretcher would be another matter. He'd need to solicit some help from the officers. He got his investigation satchel, a stretcher, and a body bag out of the van and headed down the trail.

"Hi," he said to the sergeant when he arrived. He had seen him before a couple times over the years when he was called out to investigate a death scene and retrieve a body. "I'm Kim, Deputy Medical Examiner."

"Hi Kim, good to see you again. Thanks for the quick response. The victim is over there," the sergeant said, pointing to the pile of leaves.

Kim walked over to the body, paying particular attention to every little thing around the body. He took out his camera and began photographing everything around the body. In the process he saw something that looked out of place. He got closer and realized it was intestines in a state of decay. He took numerous pictures of the intestines. Ten minutes later he decided it was time to get a better look at the body. At this point the only part of the body that was visible were the feet and the head, which was missing the scalp and facial skin. It was clearly a body, but the leaves covered the trauma.

Kim put on rubber gloves and gently began lifting the leaves and sticks away, placing them in a pile behind him. He started at the feet, observing every fine detail as he picked the pieces away, looking for tears in clothing, blood spots and anything out of place. When he'd uncovered the waist he took more pictures. He then quickly removed the remaining debris. He looked around the body. There was no blood on the ground anywhere. Generally this bit of information told the examiner that the victim had been killed somewhere else. He got down on his knees next to the victim's hands and took a close look, then studied the open chest area.

Satisfied he got up and went over to Sergeant Williams.

Sergeant Williams took a look at the body, "whoever did this is really sick."

"There's plenty of sick people around, but I'm pretty sure that this was not done by a human. Can you call State Patrol and have them send out a Fish and Game Enforcement Officer. Better inform them that we're probably going to need some tracking dogs too."

"Sure, I'll take care of that. What do you think it was?"

"I'm going to need a bit longer before I want to give you the answer to that question. I need to analyze some things to see if I can put this puzzle together here."

Kim went back to resume a meticulous cleaning off the head and torso.

When Sergeant Smith and Officer Wesson from Fish and Wildlife enforcement arrived they reported to Sergeant Williams who was in charge. Sergeant Williams filled them in with as much information as he knew.

"The body is over there," pointing toward Kim.

Kim had just finished removing all the debris and stood up to take in the whole body again when the enforcement officers walked up to him. After a short look at the body Officer Weston stepped away and heaved the contents of his stomach out into the bushes. Sergeant Smith had been with wildlife enforcement for over ten years, but Officer Weston was still relatively new. He'd seen plenty of dead and gutted animals, but he'd never seen a dead human, especially in the condition this one was in. It was very disturbing. After a few more minutes of retching he came back to Kim and Sergeant Smith, but did not look at the victim again.

"Looks to me like a pack of dogs got her," Sergeant Smith stated.

"What makes you say that?" Kim asked.

"Dogs are a problem, even if they are not pack dogs," Sergeant Smith stated. "People let them out to do their nightly business and they pack together. They're usually perfectly normal, non-aggressive pet dogs, but when they get together their personalities change. It's a developing problem around here."

"That may be," Kim responded, "but this definitely was not caused by dogs."

Sergeant Williams stepped over to them so he could gather information for his report. Two other sheriff deputies joined them.

"It was an animal that killed her alright, but it wasn't dogs," Kim stated.

"What makes you think that it was not dogs?" Sergeant Smith asked.

"Well, you have to look at all the evidence. First, it was definitely an animal that killed her. That means bear, dog, coyote, cougar or possibly even a wolf. I can't really think of another animal I'd consider. Second, the scalp was removed and is missing. That could be any one of the five animals, however it frequently happens in cougar attacks on humans. Case studies of cougar attacks reveal that the victim's scalp was frequently removed, probably in the first two or three seconds of the attack. I've never heard of dogs removing a scalp in an attack, but it could happen. The body was covered with leaves and twigs. I've never heard of that behavior in canine animals, but it usually happens with bear and cougar. More importantly, there is no evidence of teeth marks on any of the bones, except the skull. Canines chew on the tissue using deep bites that leave teeth marks on the bones."

"The next piece of evidence is the claw marks on the stomach where the internal organs were removed. That eliminates the possibility of it being canine. The claw marks are too sharp and indicate that the claws were much longer than a dog's claws. The next piece of information is the intestines, they were set in a neat pile five feet from the body. Cougars nearly always exhibit that behavior, but I've never heard of a bear doing that. A cursory probe of the thoracic cavity reveals the heart, lungs and liver are missing. Cougars usually eat the liver of their victims first because it is the body's storehouse of energy and contains a lot of vitamins and minerals. The heart and lungs are usually consumed next because they also contain a lot of nutrients."

"Most of the skin from the victim's face is missing. The peripheral remaining skin around the face is dark, indicating blood flow at the time it was removed. If it was a bear it probably would have stashed the body and then came back a few days later after it had a chance to start decomposing. Another important piece of evidence is the fingernails, there's fur imbedded under the fingernails. It's long and tawny colored. That can only happen when the victim is alive and trying to fight the assailant. Everything I see here points to a big cat attack. I won't know for sure until I do some labs tests, but that's my take."

"How long do you think she's been dead?" Sergeant Williams asked."

"It's been cool at night. There's very little evidence of decomposition or insect damage to the skin. My initial take would probably be about one to three days."

"I think this was dogs. We're practically in the city. There are no cougars around here," the wildlife officer said.

"I was a medic in the Army for twenty years. Three tours in Vietnam, one up in the mountains with the Montagnards. I saw five, maybe six victims that had been killed by tigers or leopards. The death site looked a lot like this. The information here is definitely a cat MO."

"Oh yeah," Kim continued, "one last thing. I almost forgot. She had puncture wounds on her arms and shoulders from the claws. They looked too small for bear claws, and usually bears will bite the victims in the arms and legs as opposed to using the claws there. Some of the puncture wounds in the forearm were definitely needle marks. Lot's of them, some real old. I found some on her thigh also. Good chance she was a druggie. She was wearing layers of clothes that were dirty from not having been washed for a long time. There's probably a good chance she might have been a homeless person."

The sheriff sergeant was the senior person there. "Great, that will really complicate making an identification on her."

He turned to Sergeant Smith. "Have you had any problems with cougars around here?"

Officer Wesson said, "I had a call last week from an older woman about ten miles up the river. She gave a good description of a cougar that had killed a deer in her backyard while she was gardening. Another call came from a store owner in Dual a few days ago. That's only about six miles from here."

To his deputies he said, "Let's start gathering information," and they all spread out and began to scour the area for anything that might help solve the cause of death.

Officer Smith took out his cell and called. He informed the duty officer of the findings and requested additional officers. "We're going to need some cougar tracking dogs too. I should be able to contact them from here. I'll let you know if we need assistance."

To the Deputy Medical Examiner Sergeant Williams said, "Okay, when you leave here there's going to be a lot of reporters up there waiting for a statement. The Sheriff's department will do all the talking to the press, but if they try to get a statement from you or your department say 'no comment,' or 'it's under investigation."

"That could be a dangerous position to take. This area is used by other people for hiking and walking their dogs. This attack just happened in the last few days. Someone else could get killed," Kim responded.

"I've got dogs on the way," Sergeant Smith stated. "It shouldn't take long to find out if it's still in the area. Plus there will be a lot of people around here for the next few days. Wild animals don't usually like to be in an area where there is a lot of human activity. That will give you time to complete your lab work. We'll keep working the dogs for a few days if we don't get it right away," Officer Smith consoled him. "I still think it was dogs."

"I'm sure there will be a lot of damage control for your department to contend with. I can tell you right now that I'm almost certain my report is going to say the death was caused by a large cat, probably a cougar. The fur under the fingernails is an important piece of information."

"The dogs should be here soon," the enforcement officer stated, "we'll see what happens."

Kim carefully slid the body into the bag and zipped it up. After soliciting some help from Officer Wesson they laboriously carried the body up the hill and then dropped the wheels and pushed it over to the Medical Examiner's van.

A reporter had managed to slip through the blockade by walking around through the woods. The reporter and camera man were waiting in the bushes next to the Medical Examiner's van when Kim and Wesson arrived.

"What can you tell us about the victim?" the reporter asked and thrust the microphone toward his face.

Kim looked slowly at the reporter and said, "Drop dead." The reporter jumped back. Coming from the Medical Examiner's deputy, it was a particularly ominous thing to say. He hoped it didn't come with a curse.

Kim really hated reporters. He vividly remembered the first time he'd been interviewed by a reporter. The guy had twisted everything he'd been told to make the story sound better. He hadn't given a reporter any information since.

When they finished loading the body into the van Kim thanked Officer Wesson for the help. He got into the van and started the engine. Just as he put it into gear one of the deputies came running up the trail from the watershed. He was waving his arms and looking straight at Kim. He rolled down the window.

"What's up?" he inquired.

"Think you'd better come back down, we've found something else," the officer said.

Kim turned off the engine and locked up the van.

"I'm Sal Minau," he said, shaking hands with Kim.

"I'm Kim, what have we got?" Kim inquired as they headed back down into the watershed.

"While we were searching around the area looking for anything that might help in this case we came across a human skull. It's a small one, most likely a child. Looks like it's been there for awhile. Doesn't look fresh at all."

"Just a skull?" Kim asked.

"Yeah, that's all so far."

It was pretty easy to see where it was. There were six officers standing in one place.

When they arrived Kim took a look around the immediate area. Nothing special caught his attention. He got down on his knees and took a close look at the skull.

"There's two puncture wounds on the front of the skull just above the eye orbits, about four inches apart. That's curious." He took a pen out of his coveralls and lifted the skull to get a better look all around.

"There's two similar puncture wounds through the bone below the occipital protuberance. Also, there's some marks that look like sharp teeth scrapings on the bone between the puncture wounds on both the upper and the lower sets of punctures. It takes a powerful bite to go through a skull like this."

"I think we better spread out and comb the area for smaller, individual bones. The skull has been here for months. The rest of the skeleton could be pretty well dispersed. Look under the leaves, under bushes, anything on the ground that could hide a piece of bone."

"You think the skeleton came apart?" the sergeant asked.

"This has probably been here for months. After a skeleton is picked clean the ligaments that hold the bones together deteriorate and allow the bones to separate. The animals in the area, raccoons, possums, mice, even domestic dogs on a run through the area will carry them off to their hiding places or holes in the ground. They gnaw on them for the calcium and minerals stored in the marrow of the longer bones. In some places a skeleton can completely disappear without a trace in a few months.

Four hours later three rib bones and two vertebra had been recovered. The size of each piece indicated the victim was a child.

"Can you tell if it is male or female?" the sergeant asked Kim.

"No, we'd really need a pelvic bone for that."

"How old would you guess the victim was?" the sergeant wanted to know.

"From the size of all the bones I'd guess six to maybe as old as twelve," Kim replied.

"A seven year old boy disappeared from a campsite about two miles up the river last summer," one of the sheriff deputies said. "It happened at night. The kid was playing around the campfire and apparently went out into the woods. The parents couldn't remember how long he had been gone when they started calling for him, but they said it wasn't more than fifteen minutes."

"It was about eleven thirty when we got there that night. We searched around the area for five days. Never even saw a trace of anything that helped us. There wasn't a lot of campers in the area that night. None of them appeared the least bit suspicious to us. None reported suspicious 'lookie loos' passing though the campground that day or the day before."

"It was a strange case. I was scratching my head after a couple of days. Usually if it's a pervert there's some kind of evidence. But not one camper had seen anything like that. We had close to a hundred volunteers up there. The campsites are not real close together. The one camper closest to them thought he'd heard something being dragged through the bushes behind their campsite about the time the boy went missing. It was late and he admitted to having quite a few beers that evening. He'd made numerous trips out into the woods to relieve himself. That was when he heard the dragging sound. He said the dragging stopped and something hissed at him. He decided it was time to get back to the campsite. We searched around the area where he thought he'd heard the dragging sound. There'd been a lot of people scouring the area by then. That was during the day after the boy disappeared. The ground was dry, dirt sort of powdery. Everything got displaced easily. Never found anything that looked like drag marks, footprints, nothing that helped us."

"Can you e-mail me the information and contact numbers for the parents. I'll follow up with their dentist. That's probably about the only way we'll be able to ID this victim. A case like this can be really hard. It could take months, and then maybe never get a positive ID," Kim lamented.

Kim hiked back up to the van. It was three a.m. now and the news crews were long gone. The on-site sheriff's deputies had managed to keep the new findings quiet.

Kim placed the bag of remains in the back of the van, laboriously climbed in, cranked the engine over and headed for the lab. It had been a long day and night, and promised to be even longer. Two uniquely different cases at one site seemed pretty unusual. He drove back to the lab mulling the whole thing over in his mind. As he backed the van up to the back of the medical examiner's building it dawned on him that maybe they were in fact related. That was a possibility. There was no such thing as a coincidence. He had been taught that by his first supervisor.

He deposited the body in the cooler and the small skeletal remains in the lab. He was dead tired, he'd been up over thirty hours. He figured the examination could wait a day. He'd come back refreshed, ready to pursue the answers.

Shortly after the Medical Examiner's van departed the investigation site a pick up truck arrived at the Sheriff's barricade.

"I was called out here by Sergeant Smith of the wildlife department, I'm supposed to meet with him here. I've got some tracking dogs with me. Can you point me in the right direction?"

The officer called his sergeant to confirm. "Park over there by the state patrol vehicles and go down into the canyon on that trail over there. You'll see the uniforms when you get down to the bottom of the watershed.

He parked next to the marked state fish and wildlife officer's vehicle, a rough cut man in his thirty's got out of the pick-up. Atop his head was a Stetson, under his left armpit was a .357 revolver in a shoulder holster over his Carhart jacket. He wore old jeans and a pair of well-used hunting boots. Four kennels were in the back of the truck. He opened one kennel at a time and leashed the dogs up to a four way leash tied to a single, long leash. He patted each dog on the head when it exited the kennel and he handed it a large dog bone treat. Then he headed down the trail into the watershed.

Officer Smith heard the dogs and met them on the trail. "Hi."

"Hi Jim, thanks for coming. Haven't seen you in quite a while."

"Hello Sergeant Smith. You guys finally made it worth my time with the five hundred dollar a day fee. What do we have here?"

"A body, the Medical Examiner's thinks the victim was killed by an animal, specifically he thinks it was a big cat."

"Can I take a look at the victim?"

"The body was taken off to the Medical Examiner's for an autopsy. You wouldn't want to see it anyway. It was pretty gruesome."

"Well, I was just thinking it might help me figure out what we're looking for," he took off his Stetson with his right hand and wiped the sweat off his forehead with his left hand. "I've got scent packs for bear, cougar and coyote"

The officer motioned for him to follow and led him over to the bushes where there was yellow crime scene tape staked out and a white spray painted outline on the ground around where the body had been found.

"This is where we discovered the body."

Jim led the dogs around the area for about ten minutes. The dogs sniffed and looked interested, but none got excited. He looked a little disappointed.

"How long you figure the body had been here before it was found this morning."

The wildlife officer responded, "The Medical Examiner's said probably about one to five days."

"Five days! Man, five hours is sometimes too long.

"I know, but we had to go through the

motions on this one. There's still a chance you might come up with something if the animal responsible returned to the area sometime after the initial kill."

"I can keep trying in a bigger area around here, but we'll have a lot better chance for a hit if we can give them some scent."

Officer Smith thought about it for a moment, then said, "Why don't you try using the cat scent."

"I don't have any cat scent, just cougar."

"Try the cougar then."

Jim took out the sealed bag with the cougar scent and then gave a sniff to each of the dogs. They looked up at him then continued to sniff in a larger circle around the site where the victim had been found. When that didn't produce any results Jim took an even wider arc around the trails. Officer Smith stayed back, knowing that if the dogs got any scent there would be plenty of excited dogs barking and it would be easy enough to follow them.

An hour later Jim returned to where Sergeant Smith was talking to one of the deputies.

"Well we covered a pretty good sized area from where the body was found and the dogs didn't even remotely seem interested in anything. I think it's just been too long. Time is really important in getting predatory animal scent for tracking. If it's been two or three days, that's way too long for us to do any tracking."

8

Buck was lying in a hammock that was tied up to two old cedar trees in their backyard. The trees were at the top edge of the the canyon. From his position in the hammock he could see down into the watershed below. He was reading Janet Evanovich's book THE NINES, howling with laughter when Kim Chee came around the corner of the house.

"Hey Buck, I was ringing your front door bell when I heard you laughing," Kim said. Kim lived a few doors down from the Logan family. "What's so funny?"

"Stephanie Plum's grandmother just shot the Thanksgiving turkey at the dinner table. You ever read any of Evanovich's books?"

"No, I read a lot, but can't say I've even heard of her."

"I can't remember ever laughing so hard reading a book before. They're all really a hoot."

Kim sat down in a lawn chair next to Buck. It was the one Marie usually used when they sat out in the waning light of the evening. Watching the wildlife of the canyon, and enjoying the sunset. It was very relaxing and a good way to wind down at the end of a warm day.

"Haven't seen you a round for a few days," Buck said.

"I've been working a rather perplexing case for the last few days that's kept me pretty busy. It just dawned on me that you might be able to help me. I know you're really into studying cougars. I don't suppose you'd have a cougar skull around?" Kim asked.

"No I don't, but I know a guy who might. What's on your mind? Sounds like you think you might have a victim that was killed by a cougar." Buck wanted to know.

"I'm just curious. I found a child's skull at a death site this week. It has teeth marks on it and two holes where something punctured the skull near the occipital protuberance, and two more, similar holes at the front of the skull," Kim replied.

"I can give Rick Dance a call and see if he has one." Buck pulled his cell phone out of his pocket. Buck didn't have Rick's number in the phone's address book, but Rick had called him one day last week to see if he wanted to go out on another cougar collar change with him. He had to decline because he had classes to teach that day.

He scrolled through the caller ID, "Here it is," and pressed the send button.

"Hi Buck," Rick answered after checking the caller ID. "How's it going? It was very helpful to have you with me last week on that collar change. It went really fast with your help. These new collars are working so well I'm going to change all of them. Would you like to go out on another one?"

"I would if it fits into my schedule. I've got a question for you though. A friend, who works for the medical examiner's office needs a cougar skull to use for some comparisons. Do you have any?"

"Oh yeah, I've got about ten. Different sizes, both male and female."

Buck said, "Hold on a second."

Buck said to Kim, "Yep, he's got a selection of various sizes and genders."

"Can you ask him if he has any bear skulls also?" Kim asked.

"Rick, do you have any bear skulls?"

"Yep, I've got a few. I don't study them much, but I've managed to pick up some out in the woods. I think I might have four, maybe five."

"Yes he has bear skulls too," Rick said to Kim.

"Could you ask him if I could use them to do some comparisons?" Kim said to Buck.

"Do you think Kim could use them for some comparisons?" Buck asked Rick.

"Sure, but I can't let them go out of the lab. He'll need to come over here to the office. I'll be at the lab all afternoon. Do you know where it is?"

"Yes, I remember where it is. We'll see you there about one," Buck said.

"See you then," Rick responded and they closed their phones.

To Kim he said, "Mind if I come along?"

"Not at all. I'll have to go to my office to get the evidence box. How long will it take to get there?" Kim wanted to know.

"It's up near Arlington, about forty minutes from here," Buck responded.

"My office is on the way. If you don't mind we could pick it up on the way," Kim said.

"Sure, you want to leave about noon?" Buck asked.

"Great, I'll pick you up. I still have the ME's van. I got home late last night."

At noon Kim pulled into Buck's driveway.

"Can you tell me about what's going on?" Buck inquired.

"I can tell you some of it, but not all of it. A man took his dog for a walk before he left for work a few days ago. The dog was wandering off the trail and found a body. When we were combing the area for evidence a skull, unrelated to the initial body, was discovered. After that we widened the cordoned off area and searched some more. We found two human rib bones from a child, about the right size that would go with a skull of the size we had. The skull has what looks like teeth marks on it, but there's no teeth marks on the rib bones."

"So I presume you think the child might have been killed by an animal?" Buck asked.

"It's looks suspicious, since there are four puncture holes in the skull that are about the right size for canine incisors."

"What about the original body. Was it killed by an animal too?" Buck asked.

"I can't talk about that case. It's fresh and there are some issues with it. The skull is different. Can't tell how long it's been there, but it is not a recently deceased victim. Any help I can get to ID it is fare game," Kim said.

"Hi Rick," Buck said walking through the door at Rick's office.

"Hi Buck," standing up to greet them.

"Rick, this is my neighbor, Kim Chee. He's a deputy medical examiner with King County."

"Hi Kim, I'm Rick Dance," as he came around the desk and shook hands. "Nice to meet you. So I take it you've got a case you think might be related to a cougar."

"Just curious. I've already used dog skulls against it and nothing was very close to a match. We even found a coyote and a wolf skull but none looked right. Just trying to eliminate anything that could be a possibility."

Rick took them to a room that had shelves on three walls. There was a large table in the middle of the room.

"This is where we do animal autopsies. I have the remains of all of my study cougars that have died during the study for whatever reason. We do a complete autopsy and I keep the skull and bones. I know the age, sex and weight of each of the animals. With the bears it's different. Usually it's just a dead bear I found and kept the skull, sometimes the paws. I don't have any stats on them."

He opened a box and laid the bones and skull on the table. "This is a female two and half years old. She weighed one hundred forty pounds," Rick said.

"Wow, you could put all of the bones, except the skull in a standard size briefcase," Buck commented.

"Cougars are skin, bones and muscle. I've never seen any fat on a cougar we've autopsied. They're killing machines," Rick stated matter-of-factly.

Kim took the small skull out of a box and Rick handed him the cougar skull. Kim placed the upper jaw over the skull toward the rear of the child's skull and compared the teeth marks on both the front and back of the skull against the cougar skull teeth.

"Well that doesn't work. It's not any kind of a match at all."

Next he switched the skull position around one hundred eighty degrees, lower cougar jaw to the rear of the child's skull.

"Oh that's a little better. The lower canines are close. The teeth marks on the frontal lobe are similar, but not a match. How about a larger cougar?" Kim asked.

"Sure," Rick answered. He put everything back in the box and retrieved another box. "These bones are from a female also. She was bigger. Says here she weighed one hundred sixty-three

pounds the last time she was weighed.
That was three weeks before she was hit
by a car. She was a healthy one. Nearly
six years old. That's pretty old for a
cougar in the wild, but occasionally they
get to twelve, or more."

Kim took the skull and placed the
lower jaw to the back of the head. "It's
closer at the back of the head and the
front teeth marks look better. I still
could not confirm this though. Do you
have a bigger one?"

"Yep," Rick answered. "There was a
male hit by a car up on Route two last
summer. Route two is the northern most
highway going through the Washington
Cascades. It's really remote up there,
lots of cougars and bears. The highway is
closed all winter because the snow is so
deep it's not practical to plow it. He
wasn't one of mine, but it had a collar
on it. We traced it back to a study that
was done in Cle Elum. He was twenty-six
years old. Oldest known cougar in the
wild, but not the biggest. That record
goes to a cougar killed in Hillside,
Arizona in 1917. It weighed two hundred
seventy-six pounds, after it had been
dressed. It surely tipped the scales at
over three hundred pounds."

"Can we try him?" Kim asked.

"Sure," Rick said and got out the box
of remains, laying the head on the table.
"He was bigger. He weighed two twenty
when we laid him out. The driver that hit
him went back after hitting it and took a
good look, from the safety of the inside
of his car. The driver reported that it

had a collar on it. The guy also said that he was a hunter and that it seemed to him to be an especially big cougar. That peaked our interest so we went up there and retrieved it that day."

"His teeth are in amazingly good condition considering his age. I've seen six year old cougars with broken teeth. When they start loosing their teeth it's hard for them to eat and they usually starve to death."

Kim placed both jaws into position over the skull. "Bingo, we've got a perfect match, top and bottom, front and back. Now comes the hard part. Trying to figure out whose skull we have here."

"Where was the skull found?" Buck asked.

"Well I can't tell you exactly, but it was near Dual."

"You know, I sort of remember a boy, about seven I think, went missing from a campsite last August. They never did find him and as I recall there was a pretty thorough search. Since I do cougar research I was interested because I've seen some other cases where there was cougar activity reported in the area and a person disappeared without a trace."

"That's interesting, one of the deputies at the site mentioned a young boy that went missing from a campsite last summer. He said they looked for him for days, but never found him," Kim said. "I'd completely forgotten about it. Thanks for reminding me. I'll call the sheriff this afternoon and check into it. He's not going to like this. There was strong evidence of cougar at the crime scene, but no one else wanted to believe me."

"What kind of evidence?" Buck asked.

"Can't tell you that."

"It's pretty unusual for a cougar to kill a person," Rick stated. "Since I don't know the circumstances or the evidence maybe they were just going with the law of averages. With something like that it's more likely to be a human assailant."

"There was no doubt in my mind that it was a big cat," Kim said. "The fish and wildlife agent said flatly that it wasn't a big cat. They even had hounds come in and found nothing. The sheriff took the safe side out for the reporters and told them, 'It was under investigation.' Later he told them, 'It was possibly an animal, but the cause was undetermined.'"

They put all the remains away. "Thanks for the help Rick. It was nice meeting you." Kim said as they all shook hands and Buck and Kim headed for the door.

"Sure no problem, glad I could be of assistance. It's too bad it worked out this way though. I know it happens occasionally, but it's a little unsettling. Hope it isn't one of my study cats. They do get into that area occasionally. I'm going to have to go through my records for last summer and see if any of my cats were in that area. I do have one in my study that weighs about two hundred twenty pounds and he could possibly have been in that area."

"Might be helpful. If you could place one at the scene of the crime, that would be really helpful. I'll send you the coordinates this afternoon," Kim said.

"The coordinates would be really helpful. The computer program can scan the whole data base and tell me if any of them have ever been in that area. If it turns out to be the kid camper, give me the dates. I can also search it with specific information that I'm looking for, including dates."

"Technology, I love it," Buck said. Kim nodded in agreement.

Kim took Buck back home and headed for the office. Immediately after dropping Buck off he pulled out his cell phone and called Sheriff Williams, "Hi sheriff it's Kim Chee, deputy ME for King county. I was the ME's rep at the Jane Doe, possible cougar killing last week."

"Yeah, I remember you, but I still don't think it was a cougar death," Sheriff Tate said.

"There's more evidence. Do you remember a young boy that went missing from a campsite near the Jane Doe recovery site? It was last summer, might have been in August?"

"Yep, I was there for the better part of three days. We couldn't find a darn thing. We interviewed everyone in the campground at least twice. I had a search party in the area for three days. There was no one in the campground that even looked like a suspect. Everyone that had been in the campground the day the boy disappeared was still there. No one reported anyone driving through the campground before his disappearance. People in campgrounds with kids tend to be very observant. It was strange."

"Do you remember the child's skull we found at the Jane Doe site last week?"

"Yes," the sheriff stated.

"We confirmed the teeth marks on the skull today. They were made by a cougar. We don't have a body to confirm the cause of death but, the two holes found at the base of the skull next to the occipital protuberance and on the front of the skull were probably made at the time of death or close to it."

"Great," the sheriff said.

"Can you check for me and get a name of the boy that disappeared and contact information?"

"I've got the computer up. Here it is, the boy's name was Jose Santana, age seven, good health before he disappeared. No mental problems, perfectly normal with not one single indicator. It was a big mystery to all of us that searched and questioned everyone there. Maybe you've solved the mystery. It's not so good that you think that he might have been killed by a cougar though. Don't say anything to the press about it yet." The sheriff gave all the family information to Kim, address, phone number etc.

"Thanks," Kim said. I'll let you know what I find out."

"I appreciate it." Sheriff Tate said.

The next day Kim called the parents. "Hello, Mrs. Santana? This is Kim Chee with the King County medical examiner's office."

"Have you found my son?" she asked, not really understanding what a medical examiner's office did. She had only been in the United States for eight years and still had a problem with the language barrier. She and her husband had crossed the border between Tijuana and El Centro nine years ago. It was a gruesome trek but they finally made it to the northwest with the help of friends and family along the way. Juan, her husband had found a job washing dishes at a Mexican restaurant within a few days. They didn't make much money, but they managed. Then they had Jose and his sister. The children had picked up the language easily as they played with neighbor children and by the time they entered school they seemed like natural Americans, which legally they were since they were born in America. The children spoke two languages fluently.

"Mrs. Santana can you give me the name of your dentist please?" She thought a little, why would this man, a government official, want Jose's dentist. He had only been to the dentist one time. He'd broken a tooth on the playground and the school nurse insisted she take him to the dentist. He was the only family member that had ever been to the dentist.

"Senor, why do you want to know his dentist?" she asked.

"It just a formality, it a part of the investigation while we try to find Jose," he said.

She looked in her records and gave him the dentist's name.

"Have you found my Jose?" she asked again.

"This is just routine investigation Mrs. Santana. I'll contact you immediately if I find out anything about Jose."

"Gracias senor," she said.

"De nada," Kim said.

Kim got the phone number from the directory and called the dentist's office. "This is Kim Chee with the King County medical examiner's office. You had a patient named Jose Santana. Can you tell me if you have dental x-rays for him?"

"One moment," the receptionist said. "Yes we do," she said when she came back on the line. "A full bite wing and all the molars. He's the one that disappeared last summer. Did you find him?" she asked.

"I can't say anything about that. I need to get copies of those x-rays," Kim stated.

"I'd need to get permission from one of the parents. It's the new HIPAA rules"

"This is a legal investigation of the Medical Examiner's office. I don't need permission to get the records," Kim stated.

"Oh yeah, I do remember about the legal investigation clause. I can have them ready in about an hour," she said.

"Great thanks, I'll be there to pick them up just before noon," Kim responded.

Two days later Buck was laying in the hammock still reading THE NINES, when Kim came around the side of the house. "I can hear you laughing all the way out in the front yard."

"This book is really funny," Buck stated still chuckling.

"Can I borrow it when you're done?"

"Marie's got next dibs on it, but you can have it after her," Buck responded.

"I could use a good laugh. Today hasn't been much fun. I just came back from notifying Jose Santana's parents that the skull we found was their son's. It was the first time they had ever gone on a camping trip. Not likely they'll ever go on another camping trip. Thanks for reminding me about the missing camper by the way. I'd been up for a long time when the deputy mentioned it at the recovery site. I'd completely forgotten about it. The dental x-rays matched the skull that we found in the watershed along with the Jane Doe body. This case has been one for the records."

"Sure, I'm highly suspicious that there have been other cases where people, kids or adults, have been victims to cougars and nobody will ever know. Look at this case. All you found was a skull and a couple of rib bones. It was an accident that you found the bones at all.

You take a remote area, cover the remains with leaves and dirt, which is what a cougar does. The critters of the area will chew on the bones, carry away the smaller ones to their hole in the ground and the evidence all disappears. It's been about nine months since he vanished. That's plenty of time for nature to consume all the evidence.

9

Sheriff Tate sat at his desk thinking about the news of the seven year old. He remembered that about six months before the seven year old disappeared, a forty-two year old male pharmacist from Centralia had gone missing. He'd been out looking for mushrooms, alone. He was doing research on a theory he was developing on a new medication he thought he could make from the unique mushrooms that occurred naturally in the watershed of the northwest. The site where his car was parked had been less than a mile from the body and skull discovery area. To top it off, it was thought that he had been hunting the mushrooms in the same watershed.

He looked up the number for Sergeant Smith, fish and wildlife, had given him, and picked up the phone.

"Sergeant Smith, this is Sheriff Tate. I've come up with another case that could possibly be related to the body in the watershed. It was a forty-two year old, white male, who disappeared without a trace while hiking in the same watershed. He was about a mile up from where we found the remains last week. This

incident happened just about a year ago,
but there are striking similarities to
the camper kid's disappearance. The
camper kid that disappeared last summer
was positively ID'd today by the ME. The
ME says the kid was killed by a cougar
and has backed it up with cougar skull
imprints that match the holes on the
recovered skull of the camper. I'm going
to get some dogs trained to look for
bones back up there this week. Can you
get some trained cougar dogs up there to
look around, just as a precaution?" he
asked.

"I think this is a wild goose chase
looking for a cougar in this case, but
I'll have them out there tomorrow," he
said. "I'll let you know what we find out
tomorrow night."

"Great, thanks."

He punched the intercom and told the
duty officer to get the bone hunter dog
handler set up to do a search in the
watershed for the day after tomorrow.

The next afternoon Sergeant Smith called
Sheriff Tate and informed him that there
had been no hits by the dogs on their
search of the watershed that day. In
addition, he had not seen tracks, scat,
animal carcasses or any other indication
of cougar activity in the area.

The following day Sheriff Tate assembled
four deputies and the dog handlers at the
site where the pharmacists' car had been
found.

"Okay, we're looking for remains of a forty-two year old, white male that went missing from here about a year ago. Clothes, bones, backpack, anything that might have belonged to him. We searched the area pretty well when it happened, but we need to have another look. If you come across a pile of sticks, debris, leaves that look out of place, make a thorough inspection of the area. Look under tree canopies, blackberry bushes, game trails. Use your imagination."

There were two dog handlers, Jack and Judy, a husband and wife team, each had brought one dog. They kept the dogs on a leash and descended into the watershed, along with the deputies. They both took the trail south when they arrived at the bottom of the watershed. One zig-zagged the left side of the trail and the other took the right side. They searched for four hours to the south withhout any hits from either dog.

They all returned to the starting point and then began a search in the opposite direction. An hour later the volunteer husband and wife team, got a hit from their dogs, it was a bone. A closer inspection of the bone revealed it was tibia, a leg bone, easily recognizable from any animal bone.

They alerted the sheriff deputy and the search team was assembled to the find site. They spent the next two hours searching the area without finding any other bones.

The sheriff took out his cell phone and called the medical examiner's office.

"Chee here," came the answer.

"This is Sheriff Tate, we've just found a bone that seems to be a human bone while conducting a search in the watershed just east of Dual."

"Okay, where are you?" He got the locations and directions from the sheriff. "I'm on my way," Kim Chee responded.

An hour later Kim parked the van along side the country road next to a group of other vehicles, including three county sheriff cars. He ambled down the trail and found the search party in less than ten minutes.

"Hi sheriff," he said extending his hand. "Good to see you again."

"You too, it's over here," the sheriff showed Kim where the tibia was found and the bone that was exposed.

Kim looked at the bone. It was dry, with a few animal gnaw marks.

"This bone has been here a long time, maybe a year or more."

He looked around the area. It had been a long time, but Kim had a feeling about the site. He could not place the feeling. He searched for two hours without finding anything that made any sense to him. In the meantime the sheriff and his search party had continued to search the area for items of clothing or anything else that could remotely be a clue.

When it began to get dark they all gathered together. Sheriff Tate said, "Doesn't look like we're going to find anything else here. You're sure the bone is human?" he asked Kim pointedly.

"This is definitely an adult human tibia," Kim responded.

"What do you think?" Tate asked Chee next.

"It's been here for a long time," Kim stated. "The chances of finding anything that will relate to this bone are pretty remote. Still, I have a feeling about this place that there is more to be found here. I'm not sure why, but I just do. I think I'll come back tomorrow."

They all began walking up the trail to the road. "I think you are right about the chances of finding anything being pretty slim," Tate said. "Call me if you find anything else and I'll send some deputies out."

"Okay, I'll do that," and they all went to their vehicles when they reached the narrow old country road.

It was early in the morning and Buck was in the garage with the double doors open working on his fly pole. One of the eyes had started to come loose. Kim Chee walked up the driveway. Scout immediately took off toward him barking, until Kim stopped and put out his hand. Scout sniffed.

"It's okay Scout," Buck said.

Scout turned and headed back to Buck and so did Kim.

"Hi Buck how's it going?"

"Good, what are you up to this early in the morning?" Buck asked.

"Got a problem you might be able to help with. We found a human bone yesterday in the watershed not far from where we found the dead woman and the child's skull. The bone seems to be unrelated to the other two victims. It appears to have been there a lot longer. But, that was all we found, one bone. I had a feeling there was more there, not sure why, but we looked for about four hours yesterday and didn't find anything. I'm going back up there today to look again. Do you have any ideas that might help if a cougar was involved in this one too?"

"I don't have any classes today and don't really have that much to do. How far away is it?"

"About forty-five minutes," Kim responded.

"I could probably go along to help look you look if you'd like some company," Buck said.

"That would be great. I'll pick you up in about thirty minutes."

When they arrived Kim parked the ME's van on the shoulder of the narrow road. They got out and Kim removed a garden rake, a four tined rake and a five gallon bucket from the back of the van.

Kim led the way down a very steep trail to the bottom of the watershed. On the way down the trail Buck looked around for foot prints in the trail. The dirt was soft and slightly moist, so tracks could be possible. There had been too many people using the trail yesterday for anything to be visible unless an animal had used the trail overnight.

He found a good clear print, "Look here," he said to Kim. "This is a really good raccoon print," pointing it out to Kim.

"Yeah, sure is. Look at those long toe lines and the sharp claw. Pretty cool," he said.

When they arrived at the place where the tibia had been found Kim said, "This is it. We found the bone right here."

It was about three feet away from the base of a big, old maple tree. There were still a few leaves on the ground in various stages of decay.

"This is probably a good place to do some excavation," Kim said. "We looked around the area pretty good yesterday. There were seven of us, we still could have missed something. I woke up at two in the morning last night and got to thinking, if it happened a year ago some of the evidence may had sunk down into the ground." Kim kept the garden rake and handed Buck the four tined rake.

Buck surveyed the area taking in all the surroundings, the foliage, plants, trees and the animal trails.

They began raking up the soil around the area where the tibia bone had been discovered. The ground was moist and easy to move around. An hour later they had not found anything and were getting discouraged. Buck decided to go around to the other side of the tree. It was a very large old tree with at least a twenty foot diameter at the base.

Buck scraped a layer of leaves away from the surface and began churning the soil down to about four inches deep. Thirty minutes later he unearthed a long, thin, dirt encrusted piece. He stopped, picked it up and removed the dirt with his fingers, running them up and down the curved ten inch piece that was less than an inch wide.

"Hey Kim, look at this," he said.

Kim came around the tree and took the piece. He took a rag out of a case he had brought along and a water bottle with a sprayer attached. He sprayed the item and then wiped it clean.

"It's a rib bone, looks like a human bone. It's a little too wide, and thick, to be a deer."

"Looks like it might be a good place to expand the search," Kim said.

They both started churning up the soil within a ten foot by ten foot area of the spot where Buck found the bone. Two hours later they had three more rib bones.

They both sat down at the base of the tree to take a break. "Looks like your hunch about the site was right," Buck said.

"Yeah, I'll have to bring out a team tomorrow and scour the area again with more rakes. Sometimes I just get these hunches. I don't know what it is. It seems to have turned out right this time," Kim said.

Buck looked around at the area where they had found the bones. They had all been uncovered within four feet of each other. He went over to the spot and lay down on the ground, looking up into the tree. A few minutes later he said, "Hey Kim, come over."

"What's up?" Kim asked.

"Lay down and look up into the tree," Buck said.

Kim laid down next to Buck and looked up.

"What am I looking for?"

"Look right up there at the big branch about twenty feet up," Buck responded.

"Well I'll be. It looks like a leg bone hanging on the branch," he said.

"That's what I was thinking. Can't really see anything else, but it's a big branch, probably a good eight feet in diameter. There could be a lot on top of that branch that's not visible to us down here."

Kim wanted to get up there to see what was there, but he was a little too portly for that kind of work anymore. He took out his cell phone.

"Dang, the battery is dead," he said. "Do you have a cell phone?"

Buck reached into his pocket, but it wasn't there. "I think I took it out in your van, must have left it on the seat. I don't really use it that much. In fact, most of the time I just leave it in my car."

"We might as well head back. It'll be dark before we can get anyone out here and get going on this. It's been here this long, one more day won't make any difference. Plus we'll probably need some of the sheriff department repelling experts or the search and rescue folks to

get it down. That will take a little
longer for them to get it all together."

The next day Kim parked the van off to
the side of the old country road at eight
in the morning. Other vehicles were
arriving at the same time. Kim saw
Sheriff Tate getting out of his vehicle
and walked over.

"Morning Sheriff," he said.

"Morning Chee," he said. "So you think
there is a body up in a tree?"

"Sure looks that way," Kim responded.

"I'm a little confused. Why would a
body be twenty feet up in a tree?"

"I think we need to get up there and
see what we've got. Then we can go from
there," Kim responded.

The recovery team all descended down
the trail together, following Kim. They
were carrying ropes and ladders and some
high tech cameras and monitors.

At the tree the climbers extended the
ladder as far as it would go. They
climbed up then threw ropes above to gain
access to the site where the bones were
visible. James had a video camera
strapped to his head as he climbed up the
tree. Kim set up the monitor at the base
of the tree.

James was the first climber to arrive
up above the big branch where the bones
were visible. "Looks like a human
skeleton to me. There's some bones
missing, but there's an intact cranium
with the vertebra attached, a few rib
bones, one upper leg bone and the one
full leg bone that is hanging over the

side of the limb. There's enough here to say it's a human skeleton."

Kim said, "Can you point the video camera on the site so I can take a look?"

"Sure," he switched the camera on and turned his head toward the skeleton.

"Okay that's good," Kim said, watching the TV monitor. "Can you pan it around the area very slowly so I can see what the whole area looks like. We're recording all this so we can scrutinize it later."

James slowly moved his head around looking at the whole area. Trying to see if anything looked like it was important to the investigation.

"That's good," Kim said, "Hold steady on the main site while I zoom in on it. Good, now go up the side of the trunk of the tree very slowly." Kim panned back out. "Stop, right there." Kim panned in a little again. "Look at those scratch marks in the bark. That looks like a big cat scratching and sharpening its claws and marking its territory." After panning around the area and recording everything Kim said, "Okay, it's time to bring down the skeleton."

James lowered a rope and Kim sent up a body bag, "Try to keep the remains intact if possible," he said to the climber.

James lowered himself to the big branch and locked the repelling rope so he could have both hands free without threat of falling out of the tree. Slowly he slid the skeleton into the bag, then moved the bag over the side of the branch.

"Okay, it's in the bag." He let the rope slide through his gloved hands as the body bag descended to the ground.

Kim gently laid the bag on the stretcher. He opened the bag to get a look and the rest of the group gathered to see what they had recovered. "Looks like an adult male," Kim said. "Probably about five foot ten inches, about the right size for the victim we were potentially looking for. There's an intact full upper jaw. Should be enough for us to determine if it's the person we were looking for by using his dental information."

"What about the scratch marks you said were on the tree trunk up there?" James asked.

"There was a victim found about two miles lower in this watershed a few days ago and there was some evidence that a large cat was involved," Kim said. "But this information is all confidential at this point. It is up to the Sheriff or the fish and game department to make a statement to that effect, if in fact that is my determination after the evidence is all put together. So far, neither of them have come out publicly with a statement to that effect. Neither have felt that my conclusions were totally verifiable."

The searchers all gathered and packed their gear. James picked up the rear end of the stretcher as Kim took the lead end. They all headed up the trail just as the sun began its descent into the bright red western horizon.

Near the road the trail climbing out of the watershed was steep and slick from the rain the previous night. It was about thirty feet from the base to the top of the ridge at the road. Kim was only five feet from the lip when his feet went out from under him. The stretcher went flying and Kim landed squarely on top of James, who lay staring upward at the sky.

James had the wind knocked completely out of him. In a barely audible whisper he pleaded, "Get off, I can't breathe."

Kim rolled over and James let out a sigh of relief.

"Are you okay?" Kim asked. "It happened so fast I couldn't even grab anything."

James took a deep breath. He rolled over on his side. "I think so. Man my ribs are sore though."

James got up and then helped Kim get to his feet. "Are you okay?"

The sheriff's team threw a rope down and they attached the stretcher and bag to the rope, then pulled it to the top.

"How about sending that rope back down so we can use it to get out of here. We're both a little sore," Kim said.

"Sure," came a response, and the rope sailed through the air once more landing near their feet.

"You go first," James said. "I'll follow, just in case you slip again."

"Good idea," Kim said. He took a good grip on the rope and worked his way back up the hill, James following a few feet behind, just in case.

At the top Kim loaded the bag in the ME's van and said, "Thanks for all your help," to all the party. He shook James' hand and said, "Thanks for the help up the tree and the hill. Hope I didn't break anything."

James laughed, "No problem, all in a days work. Think I'll be a little sore tomorrow though," James said.

"Yeah, me too."

10

It was Saturday morning, family breakfast day at the Logan's. Buck fixed everyone what they wanted for breakfast. For Marie it was usually two eggs, sunny side up, with toast, orange juice and bacon. Bob had four medium sized pancakes and apple juice almost every day. Wendy's favorite Saturday breakfast was waffles. Buck also had a waffle. They splurged this morning with a rasher of bacon and some mini sausages.

"What's everyone got on the agenda today?" Buck asked.

"Wendy and I have some serious shopping and lunch planned for today," Marie responded.

"Yeah, we're going to The Creek for lunch," Wendy said. "They have the best chicken salad sandwiches on rye. Mom always gets the ruben. It's okay, but I like the chicken salad, it's yummy."

"What's on your agenda Bob?" Buck asked.

"I was sort of hoping you'd come on a hike with me in the watershed," Bob said.

"Does this have something to do with your school project?"

"Yeah, kind of. I'll have to show you, it's sort of complicated."

"Works for me. I didn't have anything special going on today and it's not that often that a dad gets to spend the day with his teenage son. When do you want to go?"

"About an hour after breakfast, if that works for you," Bob responded.

"Okay, should we bring the camera?" Buck asked.

"Oh yeah, I always take it with me when I go down there," Bob said, wondering how this was going to go. He was more than a bit worried about how his dad was going to take it. But, he knew the situation was not right. The male kitten had acted very aggressive toward him again yesterday. He felt compelled that something needed to be done. He just wasn't sure what the solution was.

At ten thirty Marie and Wendy said good bye and walked through the laundry room to the garage.

Buck filled a bottle with water and put it into his fanny pack with the camera.

"Ready?" he asked Bob.

"Yep," Bob responded and they walked out the sliding glass door to the backyard and headed to the edge of the watershed.

Bob picked up the six foot long bamboo pole at the edge of the grass and led the way down the trail.

"It can get a little slippery on the trail going down when it's wet, but shouldn't be a problem today, since it hasn't rained for two days," Bob said.

"How's the school project coming along? You haven't said much about it for a few weeks," Buck asked.

"The project is going good, there's just this little glitch, and I'm not quite sure what to do about it."

"Oh, what kind of a glitch?" Buck asked.

"Well, we'll see, maybe. It might not happen today. I'm just not sure."

When they reached the bottom of the watershed Bob followed the trail down stream. New plants were beginning to emerge, but it was too early to determine what they were. They hiked for about twenty minutes until Bob stopped next to a pool of water.

"This is my favorite spot. There are so many cool things that have happened here. It's kind of like a magical spot for me." He crouched down and sat back on his heels. "You need to be very unobtrusive and still and quiet here. But, sometimes it just works and lots of cool stuff happens."

"Okay," Buck said and sat back on his heels. But that was quickly not comfortable for him. So he sat on a rock near the edge of the pool.

Ten minutes later Buck whispered, "So what is it we're looking for?"

"Shh," Bob said in a hushed tone. "You have to be really quiet and still." He was uncertain if she would show with his dad there. She had never seen Buck before. He was more than a little nervous because of bringing his dad here, but he needed some advice.

Bob sat focused on the pool and Buck did the same.

A few minutes later the familiar loud whirring sound came right behind Bob. He relaxed a little, knowing she was there.

Buck, startled at the sound, looked to his left and saw the cougar lying behind Bob. He started to jump up, but quickly realized it was purring. Bob had turned around and had his hand on its head petting it. Neither of them seemed like this was out of the ordinary.

"This is one for the books," Buck said.

"Yeah, I'd guess it's a bit unusual," Bob said.

"How long has this been going on?"

"A few months. Really caught me by surprise the first time it happened. I about swallowed my gum."

"I'll bet, but there's probably a logical explanation for this," Buck said.

Bob looked off in the distance and saw the kittens moving slowly toward them. "Well, there's more. Sit real still."

The kittens slinked in slowly from behind Buck. When they were about ten feet away the female kitten came into Buck's peripheral vision off to his left side. He turned to the left to get a better look just as the male kitten sprang toward him. Buck caught the movement and deflected the assault by swinging his left arm, knocking the kitten away.

The mother jumped up and swatted the male kitten, hissing at him and backing him down.

"That's the problem," Bob said. "That's the male kitten. He's been getting increasingly aggressive toward me for the last month. Yesterday he sunk his claws into my shoulders." Bob pulled down his shirt and exposed reddened puncture wounds on his shoulder.

"We'll need to get you to the doctor for that and get some antibiotics. Cougar wounds get infected quick," Buck said.

"Yeah, okay. But, here's the dilemma. I've been coming here for months for my project. I first met her about six months ago. She has always been completely docile and friendly. The female kitten has been the same. But, a few weeks ago the male started getting aggressive. I don't want to hurt any of them, but when the male gets bigger I think it will be a problem. I mean look, you can see backyards from here. I've been feeding her Scout's food for weeks now. I don't know where she was getting food before that. I don't know what to do."

"I've been wondering why Scout's food bucket seemed to be going down so fast. This cougar was definitely raised by a human. There is no way this behavior is normal or natural. About a year ago I was out walking Scout. We came out of the watershed a few blocks from our house and there was a house right there at the trailhead with a cougar in the window. There was a woman working in the front yard, I think her name was Jane. You put

these two things together and it makes me
curious. I told her it was illegal to
have a cougar as a pet in Washington. It
begs the question - Is it the same one?"

"So what do you think we should do?"
Bob asked.

"I have to admit Bob, it's a bit of a
surprise to me," Buck said, stroking the
cougar's back. "Kind of a cool experience
though."

"Yeah," Bob said, shoving the male
cougar away as he tried again to pounce
on him.

"We may need a little time to think
about this before we take any action. If
they have been down here for months and
there hasn't been any problems, we should
have some time. If we call the
authorities, like the sheriff or the fish
and game department it will turn into a
big fiasco. The outcome might not be what
you would like, since you seem to have
bonded with them, at least the mother and
female kitten anyway.

"This time of the year there is not a
lot of people using the trail down here,
so that should give us some time to think
of a solution. I think we should go see
Jane. It could be her cougar."

"Okay, let's go now," Bob said.

They got up and walked back down the
trail by the stream. The mother cougar
and kittens followed. It was a good sized
stream this time of year, more than
fifteen feet across. They walked past the
trail that led up to their house, on down
to another trail that led up to the lip
of the canyon.

"This is the one," Buck said, and they began the upward ascent.

After reaching the top they walked over to Jane's house, up to the front door, and rang the bell.

A few minutes later the door opened. Jane looked out, "Oh, hi," she said. "You are---?"

"I'm Buck Logan, we met a while back when I was walking my dog."

"Yes, I remember now," she said.

"This is my son Bob."

"Nice to meet you Bob," she said, extending her hand.

"You may recall when we talked last time that your cougar was standing in your window watching you work in the yard?" Buck said.

"Yes."

"Bob has been working on a school project down in the canyon and he has befriended a cougar, with kittens."

"Kittens, oh my God."

"Is your cougar still with you?" Buck asked.

"No, let me get my coat." She disappeared and quickly reappeared with her coat. "Let's go," she said, obviously excited at the news.

They descended the trail and walked all the way back to Bob's favorite pool without seeing them. Bob sat back on the heels of his shoes. "Since we didn't see them along the way, I think we need to sit quietly to see if she will come back. I'm sure she knows we're here, she's like that. She's nowhere to be seen and the next thing I know she's laying down beside me. It's kind of weird."

Within ten minutes she came walking up the trail, with her kittens. Jane stood up and Misty came straight to her, stood up on her back legs and placed her paws on Jane's shoulders, gently licking her face.

Jane wrapped her arms around her back and hugged her. "Oh Misty it's so good to see you again. And you've got kittens too."

"Her name is Misty?" Bob asked.

"Yes."

"That's a cool name," Bob said.

The kittens were rubbing against Jane's legs. Even the male kitten was behaving himself.

Buck sat back and watched the reunion, occasionally petting the female kitten. She seemed to like the attention and at one point laid down on her back for him to stroke her stomach. Purring the whole time.

"I have to admit, this is pretty unusual," Buck said.

"This is so awesome," Jane said.

"Yeah, well there maybe some not so good news," Bob said to Jane. "The male kitten has taken to some seriously aggressive behavior in the last two weeks. He attacked me yesterday. I think there's some potential problems with him being here so close to all these houses. There are a lot of kids that play down here in the summer. He'll be bigger then."

"Oh no," Jane said. "Misty is so nice.
But I'd hate to see anyone get hurt, and
I understand that's a possibility. I
tried to find a place for Misty, but none
of the places would take her. I took her
up deep into the Cascades about eight
months ago and set her free. I can't
believe she found her way back here
again."

"Again," Buck echoed.

"Yes, I turned her loose the first
time about a year ago, but not so far
away as the last time. She found her way
to my back porch in about three weeks the
first time I let her go."

"We need to come up with a plan," Bob
said.

"I'll take them back to my house while
we're coming up with a plan," Jane said,
stroking Misty and the kittens at the
same time.

"Well, that should eliminate the
potential for them getting into trouble
until we have a plan," Buck said.

Jane stood up and started walking up
the stream toward the path that led up to
her house. Misty and the kittens followed
close behind her. Buck and Bob brought up
the rear all the way to Jane's house.

At the top of the canyon Jane walked
straight to her house and opened the
door, Misty and the kittens followed her
into the house. Misty quickly headed to
the sofa and stretched out, as she had so
many times before. The kittens jumped up
and down from the sofa, over the top and
around the corners for a few minutes,

then they curled up along side Misty and quickly fell asleep.

Buck and Bob stood at the door. "Come on in," Jane said. "Let me get your phone number so we can stay in touch." She got a pen and paper and took the number. "So what do we do now? I've tried to find her a home before and came up against a stone wall."

"I have a friend who is a cougar researcher," Buck said. "Maybe he has an idea. I'll get in touch with him and see if he has any ideas."

"They seem to have made themselves at home over there on the sofa," Bob noticed.

"Yeah, Misty and I have spent lots of hours lying on that sofa."

Buck and Bob headed to the door, "I'll let you know what I find out from my contact," Buck said as they walked out the door.

Buck and Bob walked the two blocks back to their house in silence. Inside the house Bob asked, "What now Kemosabe?"

"We do what we always do when we have a problem and don't have the answer," Buck said.

"And that would be?" Bob asked.

"Google, what else? Ask Google." Buck said.

"Duh, why didn't I think of that? It's a good idea," Bob said.

"You do a Google search and I'll call Rick Dance and see if he has any ideas," Buck said.

Bob went to his room, turned on his computer and started searching the net.

Buck looked up Rick Dance's cell phone number.

"Hi, Rick here," came the answer to his call.

"Hi Rick, its Buck Logan."

"Hey Buck, how's it going?"

"Good, how about yourself?"

"Great, what's up?"

"Got a question for you. If you found a wounded cougar what would you do?" Buck asked.

"Shoot it," came the answer.

"Not quite the answer I was thinking you'd come up with."

"A wounded cougar is going to die. It's just putting it out of its misery."

"Yeah, but you are mister cougar protector."

"A wounded cougar is going to die."

"The situation is actually a little different. See, we found a cougar, with kittens, and she was raised by a human and then set free, but now she came back, with the kittens. She's living in the watershed behind our house. The watershed is surrounded by houses. It's a potentially dangerous situation to humans."

"Hey, maybe we can get them to eat some of the homeless people. That would do us all a favor, right?"

"I was thinking of something a little more realistic. Like a zoo or something like that.

"The zoo's get offers for cougars on a regular basis. Maybe it's not a big deal. Some of the cougars I study are living in similar places and they are not causing any problems."

"The male kitten is already exhibiting aggressive behavior. It jumped Bob yesterday and left some puncture wounds that will need medical attention," Buck said. "It tried to jump me this morning."

"There's a lot more cougars than there are zoos that need one. I heard about a place somewhere down near Enumclaw. It's a couple with a big piece of property and they take in animals that have been injured. They nurse them back to health and then turn them loose. That might be a possibility or they might know of a place that would take them. I think it was called Animal Recovery Habitat or something like that."

"Okay, we'll look it up and see what happens. Thanks for the info," Buck said.

"No problem, good luck," Rick said and they hung up.

"Bob," Buck called up the stairs. "Try a Google search for Animal Recovery Habitat in Enumclaw, Washington and see what you get."

"Got it, they have a nice website. They take in injured animals. Doesn't sound like we qualify."

"Is there a telephone number?" Buck asked.

"Yep," Bob read it off to him.

Buck picked up the phone and dialed the number.

"Animal Recovery."

"Hi, this is Buck Logan. I'm trying to reach the owner."

"That would be me and my husband, I'm Cory Wolfe, my husband is Frank. What can I do for you?"

Buck explained the situation.

"This is either an incredible stroke of luck or an unbelievable coincidence. My husband and I just this morning found a grant offer on the internet to take in cougars. Some big software couple up in Redmond offered a four year grant for a place like ours to take in injured and orphaned cougars. But, the grant is pretty broad spectrum. Let me talk to my husband and research the grant some more," she took Buck's phone number and said, "we'll call you back."

Bob was sitting next to Buck. When he hung up he said, "Can't say that I'm having much luck with the internet."

"That was the Animal Recovery place. We might just have a winner."

"Cool, when will we know?" Bob asked

"Don't know, she said they'd call back. If I don't hear from them in a few days, I'll call them again."

Sunday morning at ten Buck answered the phone.

"Hi, this is Frank Wolfe from the Animal Recovery Habitat, my wife talked to you yesterday."

"Hi," Buck said. "Do you have good news for us?"

"I think so. I spoke with the couple providing the grant last night and they are very excited. Could you bring the cougars out here? We'd like to meet them."

"I think we could probably do it today, I'll have to check with Jane. She's the one who raised the mother and they are at her house now. I'll tell you what, give me the address and we'll plan to be there about two unless you hear from me otherwise."

Buck called Jane with the news then called upstairs. "Yo Bob, we got the call from the animal habitat and they want us to bring them down there so they can have a look at them. Are you ready to go?"

Bob stuck his head out his door. "They're going to take them?"

"Yes, as least it looks that way. They want us to bring Misty and the kittens out so they can see them. I just talked to Jane. We're picking her up in thirty minutes."

"Wahoo! I'll be right down."

At Jane's house they decided to take Buck's SUV because it was bigger. Jane took her SUV out of the garage and Buck backed his in. Jane closed the garage door, not wanting to take a chance that the cougars might escape, and opened the door into the house. Misty and the kittens were snoozing on the sofa. Jane took some treats and coaxed them out to the garage. Misty was reluctant to get in, but the kittens jumped right in after the treats. Jane nudged Misty and she went in after the kittens. Jane jumped in and closed the door.

Buck and Bob got in the front. "What happens if they decide to get rowdy, or decide to come up front?" Buck asked.

"Good question, I've had Misty in the car before and she's never been a problem, but with the kittens too, it could be different.

"Wait, I've got an idea," Jane said and got out of the SUV.

She went to the side wall of the garage and pulled down a car gate, lifting it up showing it to Buck and Bob. The cats all jumped out of the car and followed her.

Buck and Bob got out and lifted the back gate and Jane installed the expandable gate that would separate the rear cargo area from the passenger compartment. She took more treats from her pockets and tried to entice them to the back into the read of the SUV. This time they were not jumping in. Jane crawled into the compartment and showed the treats then patted her knee. Still no luck.

Bob picked up the female kitten and set her in the compartment. When Jane gave the kitten a treat the male kitten quickly jumped in. Jane reached out and took Misty by the front legs pulling up and Misty jumped in.

Buck closed the back hatch and Jane got into the back seat and ran her arm through the side of the gate to the back and gently stroked the cats to keep them calm, occasionally handing them a treat from her ample stash.

They left Newtown and took I-90 to HWY 18 then south on HWY 169 to Enumclaw. Along the way they drew the attention of numerous people, especially children, looking and pointing with wild abandon when they discovered the cargo in the rear of the SUV.

Enumclaw was a small, picturesque town, at the base of the Cascade Mountains. The town size had doubled in the last ten years. It was on the way to Washington's biggest, and most popular ski resort. Even now the town only had a population of a few thousand. The Animal Recovery Habitat was east and south of the main part of town, which was only a few blocks long. Many of the residents who had Enumclaw addresses lived on larger, five acre and bigger pieces of property.

Cory and Frank were standing by a big barn waiting for them when they drove up the long gravel driveway. There was a huge, freshly painted, peace sign on the upper half of the wall on front of the barn.

"Hi," Frank said when they got out. They all shook hands and made introductions.

"Looks like a pretty big place you have here," Buck said.

"We have over a hundred acres. There's five acres here where we have the recovery program, but we've logged another twenty acres so we can expand the operation. We get donations from all over the world," Frank said.

"How long have you been here?" Buck asked.

"Five years. I made a killing on some internet stocks in the late 90's and another on our house in Silicone Valley in 2000." He was wearing a tie dyed tee shirt and vintage jeans, a moderate beard and longish, but well cropped hair. Cory had a long blond ponytail, with gray roots, tie dyed tee shirt under farmer type overalls and a rather large, multicolored necklace. They were both were in their fifty's and both wore knee high rubber mucking boots.

Jane opened the back hatch and the cougars all jumped out, wandered around then came back to Jane.

"This is Misty. She's a little over three years old now. And these are her two kittens. I don't have names for them.

"I've been calling the female Silky. She's really friendly," Bob said. "Never did come up with a name for the male. He's pretty standoffish." He stopped short of telling them he was downright aggressive. He figured they would find that out soon enough.

Frank and Cory stroked Misty and Silky while the male kitten wandered around nearby. "This is awesome," Cory said.

"Yeah," Frank said. He ran his hand down Misty's back. "Come on we'll show you around."

Frank led the way to the barn. It was obviously an old barn, but seemed to be in good shape. Inside everything was neat and orderly. The floor was surprisingly clea, bales of hay were neatly stacked, there were eight empty stalls. Each was clean with fresh straw or else neatly swept. A deep sink in the corner was spotless. There was virtually no odor and Buck did not notice any flies in the barn. Frank opened a door to the back side of the barn and they exited to a pasture. There was a six foot high chain link fence that went on as far as they could see. It was pretty much a pasture with grass and a few trees and shrubs in the immediate area.

"We don't really like the look of the chain link fence," Frank said. "It takes away from the natural beauty of the habitat. But, it's the only practical way to keep the animals we have inside and away from the predators on the outside. We have a twenty-four by twenty-four foot fenced in area with a top over it inside the enclosure over there," he said pointing to the enclosure.

"That's where we'll keep the cougars for now," Cory stated. "It has a small shed where they can get inside out of the weather. It should keep them plenty warm and comfortable in the winter. We plan to build a much bigger area now with a higher fence where they can roam free with more space. We've been using this space for raptors until they are ready to be set free. With the cougar grant, we'll use this space for them until we can build a bigger space. We'll build an enclosure inside the barn now where we can keep the raptors. We get a lot of injured raptors. They are usually ready to be released back into the wild after about six months, depending on the injury."

Frank walked into the enclosure and they all followed. Misty and Silky walked in and inspected the whole area. The male kitten stayed out and walked the perimeter. When Jane went out and tried to coax the male kitten in, he moved farther away from her. She tried to get closer to him, but he eluded her by staying well out of her reach.

When this didn't work, she rushed him. The others were standing twenty feet behind her, watching. The male kitten bolted. He ran to a pickup truck parked near the perimeter of the fence, jumped onto the cab and then over the fence in one smooth movement. He cleared the fence by two feet, landing on a grassy knoll and disappeared into the woods.

"Oopps," Buck said.

"Guess that's not a good place for the truck," Frank said.

"Ya think," Bob said.

"Maybe rushing him wasn't that good of an idea," Jane said.

They all hurried for the barn, going through the big sliding back door, Frank closed it behind them leaving Misty and Silky in the enclosure. They ran around to where the kitten had jumped over the fence, fanned out and looked for the male kitten. Misty and Silky sat next to the fence near where they had all disappeared into the woods. Misty could easily jump the fence, but she wouldn't leave her kitten behind. After forty minutes none of them had found it. They gathered together at the jump site and returned to the barn. Misty and Silky followed them out of the smaller, overhead enclosure, and then around the perimeter, inside the fence line.

"I feel bad about him getting away," Jane said. "He's too young to survive without his mother."

"We'll keep an eye out for him," Cory said. "His momma's here. That will be a big draw for him."

"So, what kind of financial support do you get for your habitat here?" Buck asked Frank.

"There are so many organizations out there with money for a cause. We make more here than I did as a software consultant in Silicone Valley. Last winter we spent three months at the Hilton in Waikiki. Sun and Mai Tai's. We attended four different conventions while we were there. Great tax write off. We didn't have any animals to care for at the time, so we decided to take a vacation. It gets pretty rainy here in the winter. Winters really suck here. If it isn't rain, it snow. Don't care much for the snow either. The rest of the year is spectacular. If we decide to go again this winter we'll have someone here to take care of the animals and feed the cougars. We've been talking about hiring an assistant for a year. Probably a graduate student or someone like that. A person that is very interested in helping animals."

"This grant is kinda hip man. The couple wants to come out here and bond with the cougars. This could start an entirely new era in wild animal coolness," Frank said.

"Great," Buck said. "Have them bring the kids. Cougars have big appetites."

Buck's comment flew right over Frank. He was focused on the financial aspect of a domestic cougar, with kittens, and what it could bring in with the mega-buck software types up in Redmond. There was potential for big money in this endeavor.

Buck and Jane walked to the side while Bob looked around the inside of the confined area.

"What do you think?" Buck asked Jane.

"I'm not sure. I wasn't planning on it being a money making operation, but maybe that's just reality. They are expensive to feed," Jane lamented.

Frank came over to them. "I'm going to build a bigger area for them, with a higher fence. It'll be over there," he said pointing at the area that had been logged. We'll reinforce this fence and keep them in here till we get the new area finished. Misty is perfect and the kitten is a sweetheart. What do you think?"

Buck looked at Jane, "It's your call."

Bob came over to them, "This is a nice place for them. They have a building where they can get in out of the weather too. It's all natural area. The enclosure could be bigger though."

"Yeah," Jane said. "I think it will do."

11

Kathy walked down the long gravel drive to the mailbox. She noticed a new flyer attached to the tree across the street and walked across the street to check it out. It said:

'LOST DOG'
Black & White Mixed breed
Approximately fifty pounds
Missing left eye
Castrated
Only has three legs
Goes by the name
'LUCKY'
Please call 888-5252

It was the second dog her neighbors had lost in the last few months and she didn't really have that many neighbors. It seemed a little odd to her, because she had seen numerous similar signs around the area in the last year. She retrieved the mail and walked back up to the house. She had thought about getting a dog herself, but the neighbor's dogs didn't seem to be fairing too well.

Kathy had lived in the big house for three years. She and her husband moved there from the city after he retired. They'd dreamed of having a big house in the woods for years. The profit they made when they sold their house in Kirkland easily paid for the new property, a custom built new home and a significant amount of extra money in the bank to make retirement a lot more comfortable. They'd owned the house in Kirkland for over thirty years and the value had gone through the roof during that time.

Unfortunately, her husband had been one of those workaholic types. He was not really suited for retirement. After they moved into the new house he mostly just sat around. He'd never been the type to work in the yard and he gained forty pounds in the first six months after he retired. He had already been overweight before he retired. The extra weight made it difficult for him to get around, and caused his blood pressure to go even higher. The medicine the doctor put him on to lower the blood pressure made him feel awful, so he spent even more time sitting is his favorite chair. Nine months after he retired he suffered a heart attack. Being away from the city had some drawbacks. The response time for Medic One was not as fast as it was in the city. He'd died in the ambulance on the way to the hospital.

She loved the quiet serenity of the new house. Plus the house had all the latest and greatest amenities. Double stainless steel sink in the kitchen, beautiful granite counter tops, huge brushed stainless steel double door refrigerator, tile floors, with an island counter, complete with sink. It was so much nicer than their old house. The master bath was a dream come true. The living room and master bedroom looked out at the stream and the tall, craggy peaks of the Cascade Mountains in the background.

The stream that ran across the east border of the five acre property fed the larger stream that cascaded over the lip to the canyon below. At the base of the waterfall was a spectacularly beautiful, crystal clear pool. The area was frequented by college students, hikers and fishermen all year. In the summer, when frequently in the evening, the hikers would strip down and go skinny dipping. Some of the neighbors complained loudly about the raucous behavior. Kathy waved them off as a bunch of old fuddie duddies. It reminded her of the times she and her husband had gone skinny dipping in the very same pool when they were that age. Back then there was a lot fewer people around and they usually had the pool to themselves.

Sometimes in the evenings she would take a chair out to the edge of the canyon and watch the waterfall, and at times the naked hikers frolicking in the pool below. She had quickly grown to love the place, in spite of being alone. Her son and daughter lived in Seattle. It wasn't really that far away, but they all had busy lives and it seemed like the

only time they got together was for
special occasions anyway.

She went into the garage and dumped
the junk mail, unopened, in the trash
barrel. In the house she dropped the rest
of the mail on the kitchen counter, bills
in one stack and the rest in another
stack to be looked at later. It was time
to do the weeding.

Outside she pulled her stool up to the
backyard flower bed and began pulling the
small hand rake through the soil, sorting
out the weeds, placing them in a bucket.
She loved her flower garden and didn't
mind the task. She sat there pulling and
thinking about the lost dog sign.
Wondering why she saw the lost dog and
cat signs around the area so frequently.

Over the years, as the housing area
grew out into the woods, it hadn't taken
the deer long to find out that the
meticulously tended yards were prime
foraging areas. They had become
accustomed to the people around the
houses and mostly ignored them, unless
they decided to get too close. One of the
neighbors had actually gotten one of the
deer to eat apples right out of his hand.
The homeowners found the deer to be a
nuisance because they ate their expensive
plants. The newly transplanted city
dwellers were especially chagrinned to
find that the deer loved tomato plants
and roses. It was almost impossible to
grow them, even when they were planted
inside a fenced area. Deer easily jump
over a six foot fence to get at the
delectable goodies inside. Most just gave

up trying to grow anything the deer liked.

Kathy also found the deer to be a nuisance. Whenever she caught one near the house she quickly shooed them away. None the less, her garden showed frequent signs that the deer had been there the night before. They especially liked the fresh new growth at the tips of the plant. Since that was where the flowers originated, the roses plants rarely had flowers.

Near the house, with her back to him, was a woman sitting on a stool tending her garden. The mean male crouched down next to a bush and observed the woman. He'd been watching her for over half an hour. She wasn't very active, mostly just sat there.

She got up and slowly moved her stool about three feet then sat back down and began weeding again. He tensed as he watched her every move, studying her posture. As he watched he felt that the potential prey did not present a threat to him. His tail flicked quickly back and forth. Her movement had peaked his interest.

The cougar belly crawled, inching his way closer to the woman, watching intently. Only twenty feet behind her, crouched down, his muscles as taunt as a violin string, tail twitching rapidly.

Just then a deer came around the side of the house, feasting on the yellow mums. The cougar instantly shifted his posture to his favorite prey. He took off, but the deer sensed the movement and quickly spotted him. It started to flee as the cat leapt from twenty feet away, landing on the back of the deer. The deer slammed into the side of the house, the cat quickly shifting its bite from the back of the neck to the throat in a death grip on the windpipe. The deer fell to the ground and the cougar held it by the throat until it expired.

When Kathy heard the deer hit the house she looked over and immediately got up, backing away. She watched in horror, as the cougar suffocated the deer, her mouth hanging wide open.

The cougar began to drag his prize across the lawn, then stopped for a moment and looked at Kathy, a fierce menace in its eyes.

Kathy raised her arms and yelled, "Shoo!"

The cougar dropped the deer and took a step toward Kathy. Surprised at this turn of events, she quickly started backing up toward the porch.

The cougar took two more steps toward her. Bright yellow eyes focused on her movement.

She raised her arms again and yelled. When that didn't seem to deter it she tossed her little hand rake at the big cat, just missing him.

The cougar turned to investigate the rake and Kathy backed up quicker toward the back door.

The cougar noticed her moving and began moving toward Kathy again. She opened the sliding glass door, jumped inside and just as she was closing the door the cat placed his paw inside, blocking the closure. Kathy kicked his paw out and slammed the door closed, sliding the lock down. She stood there looking at the big cat. He put his paw on the glass, realizing there was a barrier he put his nose up next to the glass. Staring at Kathy, with blazing yellow eyes he licked his chops.

Kathy jumped back, eyes wide open.

The cougar turned away and returned to his prey. Picking up the deer by the back of the neck and began dragging it across the lawn toward the edge of the canyon and the woods.

Kathy could barely believe what she had just witnessed. She ran to the bedroom and took the small .38 revolver from the bed stand. Back in the living room she saw the cougar dragging the deer off the lawn and into the woods. She opened the sliding glass door and quickly made her way over to the edge of the canyon holding the .38 in her right hand at her side. She watched as the cougar dragged the hundred fifty pound deer down the trail. She pointed the .38 at the cougar and fired. Dirt flew just inches from side of the cougar, then the cougar and the deer vanished in the foliage. She didn't think trying to follow it was a good idea.

Later that evening she called her daughter and told her what she had witnessed. The daughter dismissed the story as the imagination of an old woman, figuring she'd probably taken an afternoon nap and dreamed it, or had been nipping a little early in the day.

Most of Kathy's neighbors also had five acres, so none were close by and she didn't really know any of them very well other than to wave at them occasionally, so no one else was warned of the close encounter.

12

Bob had been working on the presentation
for his biology project for days. He had
a slide presentation to go along with the
speech. The slide presentation really
made the whole thing. The gelatinous ball
that turned into tadpoles and then frogs
were a really cool part of the project.
But there were plenty of other things.
What the watershed looked like at
different times of the year. The snow on
the trees and the deer he had been able
to photograph on rare occasions. The deer
seemed to stay up around the houses and
away from the watershed most of the time.
They seem to know there was potential
danger in the watershed with Misty down
there.

Bob walked up to the front of the
class feeling very nervous. He placed the
CD into the computer and pressed the
button of the remote and a picture of the
pool of water came up on the big screen.

"My project for the year is the
biodiversity of the area around us.
Specifically, the watershed in the canyon
that is right next to the school grounds.
If you walk through the parking lot and

over the edge down to the bottom, as I'm
sure many of you have done at one time of
another, there is a whole different world
down there. How many of you have gone
down into the watershed and taken a swim
in the stream in the summer time, or
ridden your bike along that stream
trail?" Bob asked.

About half of the class raised their
hands.

"That's about what I expected."

"Here is a picture of a pool along the
stream which I took in September. It
looks just like many of of the pools that
we have all seen when we were down there
playing as younger kids, right?"

"Okay, here is a close up of the same
pool. Look in the center of the picture.
Does anyone know what that is?" Bob
asked.

One of the boys in the class said, "I
think I've seen something like that
before, but I don't know what it is."

"I found, in this research project,
that there are a lot of things down there
that we see, but don't pay much attention
to, or we don't really sit there and
observe things closer. Here is a picture
of the same ball a few weeks after I
first saw it." He pressed the button and
a picture of the ball with the black
specks appeared.

"This is the beginning of the
transformation. The ball is bigger and it
has black specks in it. Does anyone know
what it is now?" he asked. There was no
response.

"This picture was taken a few days later." The next slide was a closer shot that showed a tiny tadpole swimming around the ball. The next slide showed a short video of a tadpole breaking away from the ball. The class oohed and awed.

"How cool," a few of the class were saying, "that's awesome."

Bob continued with his presentation showing the different seasons. The way the leaves fell from the trees in the fall, then turned into mulch and eventually provided food for the trees when the leaves began to emerge from the branches in the spring.

He had a spectacular picture that was taken on Halloween day. It had fallen on a Saturday and he had woke early in the morning. He'd decided he wanted to see what the canyon looked like early in the morning as the seasons were changing. The leaves were turning color and the watershed had yet a different beauty. He had taken Scout out for a walk with him and had taken over a hundred pictures. He showed the leaves in various color combinations and sizes. But the best picture he felt he had taken during the entire project was of a spider web, wet with dew and the spider clearly visibly in the center of the web, the dew sparkling as the morning sun hit it. The class once again drew in their collective breath when this picture came on the screen.

He also showed other pictures of the many spider webs in the area that glistened as the morning sun hit the dew laden webs. It was almost like a Halloween display in the canyon.

He had close up pictures of the leaves popping out in different stages. He had a series of shots that showed flower buds forming and then turning into blossoms, then tiny apples and plums that were growing wild in the watershed and providing food for the birds and animals that lived in the watershed.

Finally near the end of the presentation he showed a picture of Misty when she was extra large and pregnant, which he did not realize at the time he took the picture.

There was an audible surprise that arose from the class.

Mrs. Bird, the biology teacher said, "You didn't take that picture in the watershed, right off the school grounds?" she questioned.

"Yes, actually I did. This picture was taken about a half mile from the school parking lot where the trail goes down the canyon," Bob replied. "I took it near the beginning of my project. It was more than a bit of a surprise the first time I saw her. I was sitting down looking at the frog's egg mass in the little pool, when I heard this loud whirring sound right behind me. When I turned around she was laying right behind me, purring."

There was lots of commotion in the classroom. Mrs. Bird was standing at the back of the class with her hand up at her mouth, speechless.

"At first I jumped and wanted to run, or at least get away, but then I realized she was purring. My sister's cat only purrs when it's content and the cougar wasn't acting threatening at all."

Bob pushed the button and a new picture appeared, the cougar with two small spotted kittens. "Cool," came a response from many of his classmates. Bob flipped more pictures of the kittens and the mother as they grew and got larger, eventually loosing their spots. Mrs. Bird was dumbfounded and didn't know what to think.

"So I guess it's time to explain a little more about the cougar. Misty is her name and she was found as a kitten by a woman that lives down the street from me." He went on and explained more about her background, being raised to two years old, then taken to the mountains and released, twice.

"A few weeks ago the male kitten became aggressive toward me. The mother swatted him away each time it happened and she hissed at him. But each time I met them after that the male was still aggressive. Two weeks ago it ambushed me from behind and left claw marks on my arms and shoulders. My dad is a bit of an expert on cougar attacks on humans so I decided to tell him what had happened. Last week I took him down into the watershed with me. His conclusion, and I agreed, was that it probably wasn't safe for them to stay in the watershed so close to the houses, especially with the male kitten exhibiting such aggressive behavior. It seemed pretty likely that there would be problems when it grew up"

"My dad and I went on line and did Google searches and found a solution in less than a day. Last weekend, with Jane, the lady who raised Misty helping us, we took the cougars to a Wild Animal Recovery Habitat down in Enumclaw. They had a big enclosed area where they could run free and an enclosed building where they can get in out of the weather in the winter time. It's a pretty cool place. Unfortunately, the male kitten managed to jump over the fence when we went into the enclosure by jumping on the cab of a pickup truck that was parked close to the fence. It leaped over the fence in one smooth movement. I spoke with the owners of the habitat yesterday and they have not seen the kitten since the day it jumped the fence. And that's it, the end of my project, and they all lived happily ever after." At that exact moment the bell rang, signaling the end of the period.

Mrs. Bird said, "That was quite a presentation Bob." Bob's presentation, which was supposed to last ten to fifteen minutes, actually lasted the whole hour, right up to the bell. "Well done and thank you very much. We'll talk about Bob's project some more tomorrow. The presentation schedule is pushed back, those who were supposed to present today will do so tomorrow. Class dismissed," she said.

Bob earned an A plus for his class project and on his end of class report card.

13

Lynn and Ben arrived at the Small Cafe at eleven fifteen on a Saturday morning. As they entered they saw their friends right away. Waving, they walked over to their table.

On the way they passed George and Andy, who were sitting at the counter. Lynn noticed that they seemed to be intently focused in something outside the window. She looked through the window at the object of their interest. Standing on the street corner was an Asian man in his early twenties. A boom box was sitting on the sidewalk next to him and he was moving to the beat of the music. She thought it a little odd that the two men sitting at the counter seemed to be so intensely interested in the man. But, she also thought it odd that the man was standing on the corner like that. Then it dawned on her, it was a college town, and the man looked very likely to be selling drugs.

Jerry and Gloria stood up as they approached, Jerry extended his hand, "Good to see you again Ben."

"Hi Jerry, good to see you too. Sorry we're a little late. The traffic on I-5 going through Everett was awful."

"No problem, we had a tough time too, but we didn't have to go as far as you," Ben said.

"Hi Lynn," The girls embraced in a big hug. "It's so good to see you again." Lynn and Gloria had been best friends for years through middle school and high school. They were now both twenty year old sophomores in college. Lynn went to college in Seattle and Gloria had received a scholarship for track at a small northwest college two hours away from home. They were both very athletic and had been on the same soccer, basketball and track teams in high school.

They slid into the booth.

"It's great to see you too," Lynn said. "I'm glad we could make this outing work. It's been way too long."

"Will you two to be able to spend the night with us?"

"Yeah, Ben said it would be fine."

"Good, Jerry found an older student to get us a few bottles of wine and a twelve pack of Hefeweisen for the guys."

"Cool."

The waitress came over, "Hi there, what can I get you?"

They all ordered coffee and breakfast.

"Be right back with the coffees."

"Ready to go for a hike?" Ben asked.

"You bet, we've been looking forward to it all week," Jerry responded.

"Yeah, it should be fun," Gloria said. "Some of the kids at school have been on this hike before. They say it's really cool. There's a waterfall up there and everything."

On the way out of the Small Cafe Jerry said, "It's about an hour drive to the place where we start the hike from here. You've been driving for awhile already so why don't I drive us up there."

"Okay by me," Ben replied.

Jerry parked the Explorer in the small lot. There were a few other cars parked there. The guys both put on college backpacks loaded with water and snacks. Some hikers were already returning as they started up the trail.

Taking in the scenery as they walked alongside the stream Lynn said, "This is a neat place. I'm glad you picked it."

"Everybody we talked to at school said it's really a cool hike," Gloria said. "We were told there's a pool at the base of the waterfall where people sometimes go skinny dipping."

There were fir, cedar, hemlock, spruce, maple and alder trees lining the trail. In some areas there were blackberries. This made the trail an active place for animals of all types.

Jerry and Ben took the lead, Lynn and Gloria walked side by side talking about school and old times.

The mean male cougar sighted the four people from his perch high in the cedar tree. The two women lagging behind the two men caught his attention. The trail below his perch was used by both people and the animals that lived in the watershed. It was a good observation point, but it had been over a week since he had killed a raccoon. Before that it had been a week since he had killed the deer in Kathy's backyard. He cached the deer after he had eaten only the heart, lungs and liver. He never returned to that kill.

He dropped effortlessly out of the tree from twenty feet off the ground and began to stalk the hikers. He knew the area well; every trail, every bush and ledge suitable for observation and every potential attack site. Crouching down from a distance of twenty yards he crept ahead, watching the two women. When he saw four other hikers coming down the trail he retreated to an area fifteen yards from the trail, hiding behind a rock until the returning hikers passed his position. Once they were well out of sight he hurried to the trail and ran up until he could see the two women, then followed them for another ten minutes. Knowing where they were headed he left the main trail and took a smaller game trail, that paralleled the main trail, but it was concealed by growth. Running ahead until he perched atop a large boulder that looked down on the area where the two legged prey seemed to converge at the pool just below the waterfall.

"Oh, this is beautiful," Gloria said when the trail opened up at the lower end of the pool at the waterfall.

"It's a really neat place," Ben said.

"Yeah it is," Jerry said. "It's everything we've heard it was."

Lynn bent down and scooped a handful of water and washed her hands. "It's seems a bit cold."

The hikers all gathered together at a grassy flat spot next to the waterfall pool and sat down. Opening their backpacks they fished out two bottles of wine, a variety of cheeses, a loaf of french bread and some carefully packed wine glasses.

"Too bad we didn't bring fishing poles," Jerry said. "I'd like to try my luck fly fishing here. Looks like a good spot." He bent down, studying the contents of the water. "Look at this," he said pointing. "See those little things attached to the rocks? Those are mayfly nymphs. They gather little pieces of stone and twigs and attach them to their bodies until nature tells them its time to sprout wings. Then they swim to the surface and fly for a brief time to find a mate. It's really interesting to watch. When they hatch there'll be thousands of them flying close to the water. It's usually in the summer or during warm periods of time. They don't live very long so there's a lot of activity around the surface of the water. The trout and salmon fry love them. It's a great time to fish if you're lucky enough to be in the right place at the right time."

"Sounds like you've had some experience fly fishing, I'd like to try it sometime," Ben said.

"I learned it all from my dad. We used to go camping and fishing every summer. He was a fishing fanatic. We'll have to come back in the summer and give it a try. It looks like it might be a pretty good spot," Jerry said.

"It's plenty warm, seems like a good time for a swim," Jerry exclaimed. He got up, stripped down to his shorts and jumped into the glassy waters. After coming to the surface he calmly said, "Come on in, the water's fine."

Ben stripped down to his shorts too and dove in. Struggling to get to the surface, he barely made it, grasping for air.

The water was so cold it had sucked the air right out of his lungs. He struggled, swimming to the bank as fast as he could.

Once on the bank Ben quickly put on his shirt and pants. "Hey man that was not nice. That water is like ice water. It must be coming straight from the snow pack."

"It is pretty cool, even for me," Jerry said as he stroked for the shore.

The mean male cougar observed patiently from atop a rock well above the trail about fifty yards away. His chin rested comfortably on his huge crossed paws. He was high enough above the trail that it was unlikely an animal or human would see him. There was some foliage to help conceal his presence, but animals, and people, just don't look up while traversing a trail. It was the perfect place to observe and study. He was totally focused on the hikers as they sat next to the pool. He was especially focused on the two women. There was something about the way they moved that caught his attention. Occasionally his eyes grew heavy, and he drifted off into a short catnap, as he waited patiently, his senses attuned to any sound.

"Everything I have heard about this place is true. It is so cool here," Gloria said.

"We should make it a point to come here more often," Jerry said. "It's a good hike, a lot of potential for fishing, and in the heat of summer it's a great place to cool off and go skinny dipping."

"I'll go for the warmer weather for the skinny dipping, but it is a really nice place," Ben said. "Get back to nature. It's so outdoors and woodsy here. Maybe we should bring tents and camp out for the weekend next time."

"Yeah, we can catch trout for dinner, have a few brewskies, roast marshmallows and make some-mores. We should plan to do that next summer," Jerry replied.

After a lazy lunch the couples laid back and watched the clouds leisurely float across the sky. Feeling no pain from the wine they were relaxed and content.

Jerry said, "Hey look, there's a bear in that cloud, right there," pointing at a forming cloud to the south.

"Yeah, I see it," Ben said. "It's so cool that you can see things in the clouds. I remember looking for pictures in the clouds at my sixth grade summer camp."

After relaxing at the pool below the waterfall for over an hour Ben said, "Well, I think it's about time to head back to the cars." He began stuffing their belongings and trash from the picnic into his backpack.

Gloria said, "It's such a lovely place. It was a very relaxing afternoon," as they started their return trip back down the trail.

The cougar watched closely as they walked down the trail, passing almost immediately below him. When they were out of sight he jumped from the rock to the trail and began following them. When he reached a point on the trail where he could see them he left the trail and joined a smaller game trail that paralleled the main trail, but was concealed by growth. He quickly ran ahead, passing them and found one of his favorite observation points. He crouched down and waited patiently until he saw them approaching. He put his head down lower, looking through the foliage. This was a spot where the trail narrowed. It was a choke point that was only a few feet wide, with growth on both sides of the trail. When they passed in front they walked single file and were all close together. He could smell the perfume on the women. He was so close he could have reached out his paw and touched them as they walked past. He also understood that this many humans so close together could represent a danger for him, if he were detected. When they were safely out of sight he used the smaller game trail to run on ahead again.

"I think we are getting close to the cars now," Ben said.

"Hey guys, we're going to use the bushes," said Gloria. "Go on ahead, we'll catch up with you."

"Okay," Jerry said.

They left the trail and each one found a concealed place in the bushes.

The cougar crept up the trail, pressing against the bushes to the high side of the trail. Barely moving, barely visible next to the brush that bordered the trail.

Gloria emerged first, looking up the trail. The guys had disappeared around the bend.

She bent over the tie her shoe and was knocked to the ground, face first. She felt excruciating pain. Her head felt like it was in a vice. "Ah, help!" She yelled. She tried to get up, but something heavy was on top of her. She tried to shake it off by moving from side to side, but that made the pain even worse.

"HELP!" she yelled. She now felt sharp pain in her arms and shoulders, but she still could not see what was on her.

Lynn came running out of the bushes. When she saw the cougar on Gloria she yelled, "Help!"

She immediately ran over to Gloria and grabbed the cougar, sinking her hands into the loose skin just behind the shoulders, she pulled it off of Gloria and tried to fling it off to the side.

The cougar was incensed that he had been interrupted, especially that he had been touched. He whirled around and leaped at Lynn, encasing her face in his jaws, irate he twisted his head back and forth.

Lynn fought back, grabbing it by the head, trying to get it off of her. When that didn't work she put her hands into its mouth, but the jaws were clamped shut, they were like a vice. She tried to get to the eyes next.

In an instant he shifted her head in his jaws, clamping his lower jaw down on her throat. When he had a firm grip he started dragging her up the trail. Her arms flailed at his head, trying to get any purchase that would get it to release her. The cougar had clamped her windpipe shut, she could not breathe.

Jerry and Ben were running up the trail responding to the calls for help. When they saw the cougar it was about fifty yards away. Gloria was lying on the ground, motionless, blood everywhere. Ben grabbed rocks and started throwing them at the cougar. Jerry grabbed a branch that was lying by the trail and ran up to the cougar and began hitting it on the back. When that didn't work he hit it as hard as he could right at the base of the skull. On the second hit the cougar released Lynn and turned toward Jerry, but by now Ben was standing beside him. Both were yelling, Ben was waving his arms around making threatening gestures, Jerry was threatening to hit the cougar again.

The cougar hissed. Jerry took a swing, but missed. The cougar turned and disappeared in less than two seconds.

"Oh my God," Ben yelled.

Jerry went to Lynn and rolled her over. She was limp. "Lynn!" he yelled. He quickly checked her carotid for a pulse. There was none. He started giving her mouth to mouth.

Ben ran over to Gloria. He picked up her head, cradling it in his arms. "Gloria, are you okay," he yelled.

She opened one eye, not really seeing, "Ben," she said weakly.

"Oh god," he said. He began wiping the blood away from her face. "Talk to me, anything, just say something," he pleaded.

"My head hurts," she said weakly, one eye half open, trying to focus.

Jerry continued to administer mouth to mouth. He stopped and checked her carotid again, still no pulse. He began to administer chest compressions, five pumps to the chest, then two more mouth to mouth breaths, alternating this procedure. He was exhausted.

The cougar had retreated hastily. About fifty yards away, and out of sight of the hikers he jumped up into a big old hemlock tree and climbed up about thirty feet from the ground. He could see the hikers, but was well camouflaged by the branches of the tree. He watched intently.

Twenty minutes later Gloria was semi-conscious and talking coherently. Ben said, "I need to check on Jerry and Lynn, will you be okay for a couple of minutes?"

Gloria lay her head back, "Yes, go check, then call for help."

Ben went over to Jerry, who was sweating profusely. He looked at Lynn. She was pale and wan. He placed his fingers on the neck to check the pulse. Her neck was cold, no pulse. Her head flopped off to the side, no muscle tension. Ben took his thumb and pulled back the eye lid. The eye was rolled back, revealing only the white sclera.

"Oh no," he said. He pulled his cell phone out of his carpenter pants side pocket, flipped it open and dialed 911.

When the operator answered he yelled "HELP! We need help."

"Fire, police or ambulance," was the response.

"Ambulance."

"One moment please."

When the ambulance was on the way he went back to Gloria.

"Is Lynn okay?" she asked, barely conscious herself.

"Hang in there the ambulance is on the way."

"How's Lynn?" she asked weakly.

"Lynn's not so good. I hear a siren coming."

She closed her eyes. He cradled her head in his arms.

Twenty minutes later Ben saw the medics walking up the trail carrying a stretcher. "Here, over here!" he yelled standing up and waving his arms."

The lead medic waved in recognition that he had seen him. When the medics arrived they immediately went over to Jerry and relieved him of the artificial respiration. One took over the chest pressure and mouth to mouth. The other took the vitals.

Jerry fell off to the side staring up at the clouds, exhausted, glad to see the medics.

The medic taking the vitals said to his partner, "There's no pulse, no respiration, even after all the artificial respiration, she's pale and cold to the touch. It's too late."

"I figured that would be the case when I saw her," the other responded. Looking over at Jerry he said "I'm sorry, we can't help her."

They went over to Gloria. Checking vitals they found she was stable, "Hello, can you hear me?" One of the medics said as he stroked the side of her face.

She opened her eyes, just a small amount. "Yes, I can hear you," she responded weakly.

Where does it hurt?" he asked.

"My head, it's throbbing," she responded.

He pulled a small envelope sized container out of his bag. "Where does it hurt, can you put your hand on the spot?" he asked.

She placed her hand on a spot near the temple.

The medic twisted the bag, which immediately began to get very cold, and pressed it on the spot she had indicated. He noticed there were numerous, bleeding puncture wounds all over her head.

"Oh, that feels much better," she sighed with relief.

The other medic pulled out his cell phone and called for another Medic One unit. He also told the dispatcher that there had been a cougar attack and to call the state patrol, the sheriff department, the county medical examiner and the fish and game department.

Ten minutes later vehicles began arriving at the parking lot. In another ten minutes the area was crawling with people. The ME began taking in the information around Lynn, while a female deputy sheriff tried to console Jerry.

When the extra people began arriving at the attack scene the cougar climbed down the tree and made a hasty retreat up the trail and through the brush.

14

Buck and Bob stood in the garage studying their fly rods and trying to decide what to put in their fishing vests for the afternoon fishing trip up in the mountains.

"What kind of flies do you think we'll need?" Bob inquired.

"Hard to tell, we better take a variety of flies from size fourteen to twenty. Try to separate them as much as possible in the round plastic compartments. We'll have to look at the water when we get there to see what types of insects are active. If we don't find anything that looks promising, we'll just have to use the trial and error method."

"Ok, there seems to be plenty of choices in this display box. You've really had this box a long time, but it's still in good shape."

"Grandpa gave me that box of flies for my birthday when I was about your age. It had a bunch of varieties in it. The original flies are all gone now, but it's a nice box, a lot of cork strips to stick flies in. I try to keep the smaller sizes at the top and work down to the size twelve's at the bottom.

Bob selected a folding knife from the bench and slid it into his pocket so the side clasp attached to his front pants pocket making it easily accessible. It had a knob on the side of the blade so it could be opened with one hand and locked into place once fully extended.

They stowed all the equipment in the back of the SUV.

"I almost forgot the survival pack," Buck said, and grabbed it off the hook on the wall, placing it in the SUV with the rest of the equipment. "Looks like that's about it."

They went into the kitchen and made lunches, filled water bottles and made a last pit stop. Buck said, "Let's get some jackets, just in case. It's nice here right now, but you never know in the northwest when it will start raining."

They went into the laundry room and each selected a hooded, mid weight jacket. Buck took a broad brimmed, dark, dull green felt hat that was loaded with a variety of flies, Bob took a WSU ballcap.

It was just under an hour ride to the parking place, nothing more than a pull out along side the road. "It's about a ten minute hike from here to the stream, then another ten or so minutes to the falls. The pool at the bottom of the falls is a beautiful spot, as I remember and it used to be good fishing. If it doesn't produce we can hike up the side of the falls and try it upstream," Buck said.

"It's a nice day, should be fun even if we don't catch anything," Bob declared.

"Yeah, it's always nice to be out in the woods on a beautiful day in the northwest. Smell that crisp, fresh evergreen. I've always loved that smell since I was a kid," Buck observed. "There's something about certain odors that you remember all your life. Sometimes odors remind you of special places."

"Yeah, I love that smell too. It's really unique," Bob observed.

When they reached the falls there were two couples just packing up their picnic things getting ready to hike back out. They had noticed an SUV parked in a lot on their way up the hill. They had a good hour to hike back to their car Buck thought. Buck waved at the couples as they made their way around to the far side of the waterfall.

They found a nice deep pool near the base of the falls. The water was crystal clear and they could occasionally see a nice big trout swimming in and out of the rock cover, trolling for a snack. The bottom looked to be about fifteen feet deep, but pools of water can be deceptive. The pool was in a backwater from the base of the falls where it was relatively calm and out the main flow, as the water left the pool and flowed out to the stream heading down the canyon.

"I'll try a size sixteen caddis fly
first, why don't you try something else
and we'll keep switching till we find
something that they like," Buck
suggested.

"Ok, I'll try a size eighteen
wollybugger," Bob declared.

Bob tied the fly onto the tapered end
of his line and began to play out the
spool, flicking the fly back and forth,
letting out a little at a time. When he
felt he had enough line out he dropped
the fly in the water at the far end of
the pool. It stayed on the surface and
drifted with the flow. When it reached
the lower end of the pool, Bob pulled the
line in, hand over hand until it was
close enough to begin the casting
sequence again. After a dozen casts the
fish had shown no interest in either of
their offerings.

"Not much interest on mine," Bob said.

"Mine either," Buck replied. "Now that
the flies are getting soaked they will
start to drift lower. You can see that
the fish seem to be staying closer to the
bottom. It's still a little early in the
afternoon. Later they will come up to the
surface. We need to get the flies down to
where the fish are."

Bob put a very small split shot on his
line about three feet from the fly and
tried again. This time he could see the
fly dropping toward the bottom shortly
after it hit the water.

Near the center of the pool a huge
trout came out of the rocks at the bottom
of the pool and ripped his line. Bob held

the tip of his pole up to keep tension on the line. He gave it enough slack to run, but not enough to get tangled up under the rocks. He slowly began to pull in the line as the trout began to tire. When he got it near the surface, the trout spotted him and took off. Ten minutes later he landed it.

"That's a nice rainbow Bob," Buck observed as Bob held it gently at the waters edge.

"Should I keep it?" Bob asked.

"We can only keep four between us, and we're just getting started. It's up to you."

"It is a nice one, probably close to twenty inches. Think I'll let it go though so we can fish longer."

Bob gently removed the hook with a small pair of needle nosed pliers then moved the fish back and forth until it took off for the bottom.

"I've got one!" Buck said. He played the fish out until it tired then slowly drew it in. Each time he got the fish within about twenty feet of the shore it took off for deep water. Buck had to let it run or it would break the line. After ten minutes and numerous repeated runs Buck eased the fish to the edge.

"Wow, I've never seen one like that. What is it?" Bob asked.

It's a brook trout. You don't see many of these anymore. In fact, when I was a kid you didn't see many then either."

"It's not as big as mine was," Bob said. "Are you going to keep it?"

"No, brook trout are too rare. I'll leave it for someone else to catch some day," Buck said as he eased it back and forth, letting it rest and forcing water through its gills. Slowly, it eased out of his hands and swam leisurely to the bottom of the pool and disappeared behind a big rock.

"Look, right over there at the far edge of the pool" Buck said. "See that little swirl?"

"Yeah, what is it?"

"It's a trout coming to the surface to slurp in an insect. You have to watch real close to see things like that because they are not real obvious," Buck said. "Cast your fly just above the swirl and see what happens."

Bob worked his line back and forth and dropped the fly in the water about ten feet down flow from the ripple. He quickly flicked the fly out of the water and let out more line. The fly dropped about five feet above the swirl, right in the same place as the ripple started. Bob immediately felt a slight tug at the line. He flicked the tip of the pole ever so slightly and the fish was on. It took off for deep water.

"Keep the tip up and give him some run, but not so much he can get to the bottom and get tangled up in the rocks or whatever is on the bottom," Buck instructed.

Bob played the fish for about seven minutes until it finally gave up and allowed itself be pulled into shallow water. He gently removed the hook and let it swim away. "That was a nice one," Buck said. "Looked a little bigger than the last one."

"Yeah, maybe twenty-two, twenty-three inches."

"Oh look," Buck observed, pointing across the pool to the far side. "See that line forming, looks like a feather fanning away from the point," Buck said, flipping his line back and forth, he dropped the fly about six inches in front of the point.

The point of the feather trail began advancing rapidly. Buck gave a quick flick of the tip just as the point reached the fly. The pole rapidly bent and Buck let out the line to keep the fish from snapping the one pound test line. He played it for ten minutes until it tired out and he was able to get it close enough the remove the hook.

For the next half hour, neither of them had a bite. Buck opened the snack pack and pulled out two sandwiches. "Here," as he handed one to Bob and they both sat back and watched the waterfall cascading down the cliff.

"This is a cool place," Bob said. "How come we've never been here before?"

"I'd forgotten all about it until Rick Dance mentioned it a few weeks ago. I've only been here a couple of times before. It's a long way from where I grew up.

When they finished their sandwiches and put the wrappers into the backpack Buck said. "Let's hike up above the falls and try it up there. We've got a few hours before dark. That will give this pool a rest for awhile. If we don't get any to take home up there we can stop here on our way back to the car before dark."

"Sounds good to me," Bob said as he gathered his gear.

When they were walking up the trail alongside of the falls there was a loud crashing noise. Something was running through the brush. They stopped to listen. It passed them, unseen through the dense foliage.

"What was that?" Bob asked.

"I don't know, but from the sound, it was fairly large."

"Seems to be gone now. Sounds like it's headed up to the top of the falls."

"Let's take a look," Buck said.

They found a deer trail heading through the foliage in the direction where the noise came from. About fifteen feet from the main trail, it paralleled the primary trail that led up to the top of the falls. Only this one was not as open. This trail led through foliage with an opening that was about five feet high.

"What do you make of this?" Bob asked.

"It's about the right size for deer, about five feet high and three feet wide. It could also be used by other animals, like raccoons and coyotes."

"And cougars," Bob noted.

"Yeah, cougar too."

Two minutes later they heard two loud bangs.

"That sounded like a gun," Bob observed, a little alarmed.

"Sure did," Buck said. "We need to be careful if there is someone shooting up there."

When they reached the top of the trail there was an older woman standing at the edge of her back yard. A pistol in her right hand hanging at her side.

"Hello there, don't shoot," Buck yelled.

"Howdy," the old lady said. "Damned cougar, scared the crap out of me last week. Keeps hanging around like a bad penny."

"A cougar you say. Are you sure it was a cougar?" he asked.

"Oh yeah, it's a cougar all right. Killed a deer last week while I was pulling weeds. Right over there," she waved the pistol toward the side of the house. Ran past me so close I could feel the breeze. Slammed the deer right into the side of my house. I stood there with my mouth hanging open as I watched it dragging the deer across the lawn. Then it saw me and dropped the deer, started slinking toward me. That got my attention right away," she said.

"What happened then?" Bob asked intently.

"I started backing slowly toward the sliding glass door, over there," she waved the pistol at the door. "I could tell that I wasn't going to make it before it got to me. So I flung my little hand rake toward it. The cougar pounced right on it. Gave me a chance to bolt for the door. Just made it too. The door wasn't even closed by the time it was there. Put it's paw right inside the last few inches of the door. I kicked it back out with my foot and slammed the door closed."

"What happened next?" Bob asked.

"That was the kicker," she said. "We stood there face to face. I mean it was on the other side of the glass, but only inches from my face. Then it licked it's chops, twice. Like to give me a dang heart attack."

"Did you call the fish and game department?" Buck asked.

"I called the sheriff. A deputy showed up in about ten minutes and a fish and game officer showed up about an hour later. The deputy looked around and couldn't find it. About the time he got back here the fish and game officer showed up. The sheriff turned it over to the game guy and took off. The game guy looked around and found the drag marks. He disappeared down the trail and came back about an hour later. Said he followed the drag marks till they were no longer visible. He brought some dogs out the next day and they were out there all day, but didn't find anything. He gave me his card and said to call him if it came back."

"You probably should call him now. In the mean time, I have a hunting license with a cougar tag, but I don't have a gun with me."

"Here, take this one," she said, handing Buck the butt of the .38 caliber pistol, barrel pointing down.

Buck flipped the cylinder open and extracted the two empty cartridges. "Do you have any more shells?" Buck asked.

She reached into her apron pocket and handed Buck a hand full of shells. Buck loaded and flipped it shut.

He looked at Bob, "Want to go or stay here?" Buck asked.

"Are you kidding? I'm going."

They laid their fishing gear down on the lawn.

"We'll go take a look and see if we can find it," Buck said to her. "Call 911 and ask for state patrol. That will get the fish and game officer here faster."

They headed to the trail along side the stream until they came to a trail that branched off away from the stream. This was more of a game trail. Buck looked at the ground closely.

"See this?" Buck pointed.

"What is it?" Bob asked.

"Look closely, here is a pad print and there are two toe prints. They are barely visible, but it's a cougar print."

They took the game trail. It was not as easy to negotiate.

The cougar lay resting in the brush beside the trail. He had run for nearly a mile. He needed a break. Then he heard something coming up the trail.

Buck half heard and half sensed something. In one fluid motion he spun to the left raising the pistol in his right hand. The cougar was in the air when he pulled the trigger. It was five feet away. He raised his hand and struck the cougar just behind the head on the upper right shoulder deflecting the cougar off to the right.

Buck looked down at the ground, "Damn," he said.

Bob grabbed his shoulder, "Are you all right?" he asked.

"Yeah, I'm okay," he said, studying the ground.

"What is it?" Bob asked.

"Look, blood."

"Oh good, you hit it."

"Actual, that may not be so good," Buck said. Bob had never been hunting before.

"Why?" Bob asked.

"Cougars, and bears for that matter, don't like being shot."

"Guess I wouldn't like it either," Bob responded.

"The problem is they can get really bad tempered when they're wounded. Now we have to track it down. That can get dicey."

"Oh," Bob said. "Maybe we should get some help."

"We really need to solve this problem now," Buck stated. "Be alert and ready for anything. I'm going to be scanning out in front of me. You look at the ground occasionally for traces of blood, but don't let your guard down. Be especially aware of sounds."

Bob pulled the knife out of his pocket and flicked it open.

Buck led the way up the trail. It began to narrow.

"Here's a spot of blood here," Bob said.

Buck examined the spot. "Good eye Bob, it's not much, but it's blood all right. Looks like it isn't bleeding much, or the fur is absorbing it."

The mean male ran up the trail for about fifty yards then left the trail into the cover of denser brush. He stopped momentarily to lick his wound. The bullet had entered his shoulder just above the bone and exited through the skin, missing the bone and leaving clean entry and exit holes. He found the smaller game trail that paralleled the main trail and headed back down toward the humans. The trail was smaller, probably used by smaller game like raccoons, possum and rabbits. In some places he had to belly crawl to pass through. When he heard the humans passing on the main trail he stopped, hunkered down and listened.

When he was sure they were farther up the trail he moved back to the main trail and began to follow them. He moved slowly then fast until he had them in sight. Belly crawling, he advanced on the humans until he was tracking twenty feet behind them.

"Hey dad, look here," Bob exclaimed. "There's blood going off on this smaller trail."

Buck stopped and turned around just in time to see the cougar flying toward them. He shoved Bob to the left with his left arm raising the pistol with his right hand.

The bullet struck the cougar at the base of the neck, just above the breast plate.

Buck raised his left hand just in time to catch the left side of the cougar's face and push it away an instant before the jaws snapped shut. Buck was flat on his back and the cougar was on top of him. It whipped its head back to the right, opening his jaws to go for Buck's head. Buck's right hand was pinned underneath the cougar. He raised his left hand to fend off the next onslaught.

Bob thrust the blade to the hilt into the base of the cougar's neck. He violently yanked the blade to his left. The serrated edge of the blade near the hilt sliced through the tough cougar hide and severed the jugular vein. Blood spurted everywhere.

Bob put his right foot on the side of the cougar's chest and shoved it off of Buck. Amazingly, the cat was still alive and madder than ever. It came back at Buck again, jaws wide open for an attack on his face.

Bob thrust the knife into its back just behind the head in the space between the shoulder blades, severing the spinal column. Buck rolled to the left and fired into the cougar's side at the same time. The cougar dropped in a limp pile.

Buck flopped over on his back, looked up at Bob and let out a sigh of relief. "Thanks," wiping the blood from his face.

"It all happened so fast," Bob said. Looking at the cougar Bob observed, "Man he's huge."

Bob helped Buck get up. Nose to the tip of his tail looked to be about at least eight feet. "Yeah, probably over two hundred pounds," Buck figured.

Just then two fish and game officer's arrived. "I heard the shots," one said. "Are you two OK?"

"I think so. He came in from behind us and caught us by surprise," Buck said.

The officers took a good look at the cougar, "You're lucky," said one of the officers. "A young woman was killed by a cougar about an hour ago down below the falls and another is on the way to the hospital. She's in pretty bad shape. It seems likely that this is the one responsible. Cougar attacks on people are very rare."

Buck looked at the officers. The one in front wore Sergeant's stripes. His name tag said Smith. The other's name tag read Wesson.

Sergeant Smith said, "Do you have a hunting license?"

"Yes, as a matter of fact I do," Buck replied. "Does it make a difference? You said this cougar just killed someone."

"Can I see it please?" Smith asked.

Buck stuck the .38 in the back of his waist band and fished the license out of his vest pocket.

"I see you got the full ticket, fishing and hunting, with the cougar, bear, deer and elk tag. Do you have the tag with you?" he asked.

"No, I wasn't planning on doing any hunting today. It just sort of happened by accident. An old lady was shooting at it when we came up the trail at the top of the falls. We were actually fishing, but she said the cougar had killed a deer right next to her as she was gardening last week and she didn't like it hanging around waiting to make a meal of her. I offered to take a look and she handed me her gun."

"Yes, I was out here to check on it myself last week. Ran the dogs all day and came up with nothing. When you live out in the woods you have to expect there to be wildlife around," Officer Wesson stated.

"I see the weapon you used is legal for killing a cougar." Sergeant Smith said. "Under the circumstances I'll let the tag go this time."

"You mean you'd write me a citation?" Buck asked incredulously. "A woman was just killed by a cougar and there was an incident here less than a week ago."

"Just doing my job," he stated. "The animal rights activists scrutinize everything we do. Whenever a cougar gets killed they are right there. They want to know why it was killed. The fact that it may have killed a human is of no concern to them. Some of them are really fanatics. But, they are taxpayers too, and everyone seems to get their say."

"Pretty hard to believe," Bob said.

"I spent twenty years in the US Navy protecting our country and our freedom." Buck said. "It's a great country.

Everyone has a right to their own opinion, no matter how wrong it is.

"So do we get to keep the cougar?" Bob asked. "I think I'll hang it on my wall."

"I understand that this is a legal kill and you have the license and all. However, this cougar is evidence as the possible cause of the woman's death. We'll have to take possession of it and take it to the lab for analysis."

"Do we get to keep it after you're done with it?" Bob asked, disappointed.

"Possibly, but don't hold your breath waiting for it. There is potential for a lawsuit because of the uniqueness of the attack and the death. This sort of thing could take years to come to an end. We'll have to keep it in the evidence locker until we're certain that the incident is closed."

"What happened?" Buck asked.

"We were at the scene starting an investigation when the dispatcher notified us that Mrs. Carlson had called in the cougar in her backyard again. It seemed likely that it was the same one, so we got up here as fast as we could. We've called for tracking dogs, but they haven't arrived yet. We'll still use them when they get here, but this is likely to be the one. Since it's a male it isn't likely there will be another around."

"Anyway, to answer your question, apparently there were four hikers who had separated temporarily. The two men had gone on ahead. One of the women was attacked out of the blue. None of them had seen the cougar prior to the incident."

"It attacked one of the women from behind. Apparently the other woman then grabbed the cougar and tried to pull it off her friend. The cougar turned on her instantly and had her face in its jaws in a vicious assault. The cougar twisted its head back and forth and began dragging her away. From the account it sounded like the cougar was mad at being interrupted from the first victim."

"The two men heard the screaming and came running back. One of the men found a large tree branch lying on the ground, it was about three feet long. He picked it up and hit the cougar in the back of the head with all his might. It took two blows before the cougar let go and ran up the trail."

"Wow," Buck said. "He is a big one."

"Yes he is," Sergeant Smith said. "I don't believe I've ever seen one this big before. He must be getting plenty to eat to have grown to this size."

Buck looked at Bob. "Guess we might as well take off."

"Yeah, too bad we don't have a camera," Bob said. "At least we'd have a picture."

Officer Wesson said, "We'll have plenty of pictures before this is over. I'll send you some."

"Cool!" Bob said. "Oh wait," he pulled his cell phone out of his pocket and began taking pictures. "The quality isn't as good as a regular digital camera, but it will do. At least I can prove to my friends that we really did kill a cougar. Mom and Wendy will be impressed too."

When they reached the old lady's house she was sitting in a lawn chair at the edge of the grass watching the falls, a drink in her hand. She got up, a little unsteady on her feet.

"I heard the shots. Did you get him?" she asked.

"Sure did," Bob reported. "He was a big one too. The fish and game sergeant said he'd never seen one that big before."

"Well I'll be," she said.

"Why don't you sit back down," Buck suggested. Pulling the .38 out of the back of his waistband he flipped the cylinder open and pressed the rod, ejecting the shells into the palm of his right hand.

"Thanks for the use of the pistol. Good thing we didn't go in there without it," he said, handing her the butt of the pistol and dropping the shells into her other hand.

"I'm Buck Logan by the way. This is my son Bob."

"Kathy Carlson's my name. Nice to meet you young fellas. I appreciate you getting rid of that dang cougar. Haven't felt comfortable doing my gardening since that thing killed the deer right next to me. Would you two care for something to drink? You could probably use something after that excursion. I've got sodas, iced tea, and lemonade." she asked.

"Ah, no, but thanks anyway, think we'll have to pass. It's about time for us to head back to the car before it gets dark," Buck said as he reached down and retrieved his fly rod. Bob followed suit.

"You're probably parked just down the road by that wide pull out. I can give you a ride if you'd like," Kathy said.

Buck thought for a second, "Thanks for the offer, but we'll be fine hiking out."

As they headed toward the trail Kathy said, "Stop in and say 'hi' next time you're up here fishing."

"Okay, we'll do that," Buck said and they waved back at her.

When they got to the pool at the base of the falls Buck stopped, looking at the spot where they had caught the fish earlier in the day. "Want to see if we can catch a couple to take home?

"Naw, I think I've had about as much excitement as I need for one day."

It took another twenty minutes for them to reach the SUV. On the way down the hill they passed the parking area for the lower trail. There were four sheriff vehicles, two state patrol cars, the medical examiner's van, three media vans with satellite dishes on top and an assortment of other vehicles. It was just starting to get dark, but the flood lights were already fired up illuminating the path.

Marie and Wendy were in the kitchen when they walked in from the garage.

"How was your day?" Marie asked.

"Are we having trout for dinner?" Wendy asked.

"Not tonight," Buck responded.

"You won't believe what happened to us today," Bob said. He grabbed a soda from the refrigerator and sat down at the kitchen table. He took out his cell phone and began to tell the tale, showing them the pictures as the story unfolded.

EPILOG

The media reporting coverage on the death of Lynn at the falls trail was intense. Cougar sightings were reported all over the state for weeks following Lynn's death. Each of these sightings was covered by the media. Two weeks later Gloria died in the hospital. The cause of death was listed as uncontrollable cerebral infection. What wasn't stated was that it was caused by the cougar's canine teeth puncturing the cerebrum. This caused a new wave of the media reporting on cougar behavior across the west.

During this time a reporter interviewed a clean-up crew worker at the county medical examiner's office. He vaguely stated that he thought there were other recent cougar related deaths, indicating the Gretchen Wortz case and what had evolved from that search for evidence.

In a direct interview with the Medical Examiner herself, she admitted that there was some evidence that the death of Gretchin Wortz could have been caused by a large, predatory animal. Over the next few days the media slowly uncovered the possibility that the death of the seven year old camper and the forty-two old pharmacist from Centralia may all be related.

Lawsuits eventually were filed by the families of each of the victims. In the years that followed each suit was settled

at a cost of over five million dollars,
each.

This book is fiction. The behavior exhibited by the cougar named Misty in this book will not happen in real life. Cougars are very dangerous animals. It is believed by some that one of the fatal attacks that occurred in the 1990's happened because the victim tried to approach the cougar.

If you are confronted by a cougar, make eye contact and back away, wave your arms, stand up tall and yell at it. Get everyone there close together. Pick up children. Throw rocks at it. Try to make it go away.

If a cougar attacks you, fight for your life, it intends to eat you. Use anything you have, a knife, a stick, anything.

A hiker in Colorado who was attacked had nothing to use, so he stuck his finger into the cougar's eye socket and pulled the cougar's eye out. It saved his life.

WORLD RECORDS

COUGAR
"The largest North American cougar ever killed in the wild was taken by J. R. Patterson, a government hunter of predators, near Hillside, AZ, March 1917. This cougar weighed 276 pounds even after the intestines had been removed."
(*COUGAR*, By Harold P. Danz, 1999, Swallow Press/Ohio University Press, Athens, Ohio, Page 44.)

BOONE & CROCKETT WORLD RECORDS

COUGAR
Score 16 4/16
Tatlayoko Lake, B.C.
Hunter Douglas E. Schuk
1979
Key Measurements
Greatest length of skull without lower jaw 9 9/16
Greatest width of skull 6 11/16

Jaguar
Score 18 7/16
Sinaloa, MX
Hunter C. J. McElroy
1965
Key Measurements
Greatest length of skull without lower jaw 10 15/16
Greatest width of skull 7 8/16

(boonandcrocket.com)